The Catalans

UNIONTOWN PUBLIC LIBRARY

MEMORIAL BOOK

PATRICK O'BRIAN

The
Catalans

THORNDIKE
WINDSOR

This Large Print edition is published by Thorndike Press®, Waterville, Maine USA and by BBC Audiobooks Ltd, Bath, England.

Published in 2006 in the U.S. by arrangement with W. W. Norton & Company, Inc.

Published in 2006 in the U.K. by arrangement with HarperCollins Publishers.

U.S. Hardcover 0-7862-8415-3 (Famous Authors)
U.K. Hardcover 1-4056-1406-4 (Windsor Large Print)
U.K. Softcover 1-4056-1407-2 (Paragon Large Print)

The text of this Large Print edition is unabridged.
Other aspects of the book may vary from the original edition.

Set in 16 pt. Plantin by Christina S. Huff.

Printed in the United States on permanent paper.

British Library Cataloguing-in-Publication Data available

Library of Congress Cataloging-in-Publication Data

O'Brian, Patrick, 1914–
    The Catalans / by Patrick O'Brian.
        p.   cm. — (Thorndike Press large print famous authors)
    ISBN 0-7862-8415-3 (lg. print : hc : alk. paper)
    1. Catalonia (Spain) — Social life and customs — Fiction.
2. Large type books.   I. Title.   II. Thorndike Press large
print famous authors series.
    PR6029.B55C47 2006
    823'.914—dc22   2005033425

For Mary, with love

Chapter One

At Carcassonne the carriage emptied, and until Narbonne Dr. Roig had the compartment to himself. He was glad of it, for although his companions had been agreeable men and women he was feeling too stupid and bleary at this time of day — the hour of dawn, after a long night's run — far too stupid to talk.

They wished him a good journey, he bade them farewell; and when the train pulled out he sank luxuriously into the corner seat: it was the first time since he had climbed into the train that he had been able to sit easy, spread out, uncramped, and he promised himself a quiet doze for an hour at least. On his right the great dark bulk of the Cité soared up, its fantastic battlements sharp against the pale sky: it revolved slowly, a half-turn, and slid away into the corner of the window as the train gathered speed. He leaned forward, straining his eyes to catch the last glimpse as it vanished, and then, easing himself back into his corner, cushioned against the rhythmic swing of the train, he closed his eyes.

In the corridor, a man, overburdened with parcels, a string-fastened suitcase and a basket with a duck peering from it, battled his way slowly down the train on some laborious errand: with every swing of the carriage he lurched against the outer window or an inner door, and as he banged against the doctor's compartment he cried "Mare de Deu de Deu de Deu de Deu. Boun Deu, Senyor." At the sound of the Catalan Dr. Roig opened his eyes: it was his mother tongue, and although he had not used it for so many years, still he dreamed in Catalan. The sound of it brought the end of his journey clearly into the immediate present; a long journey, from the confines of Prabang, weeks of traveling, half across the world: but now suddenly the end was in sight, so near that he could touch it. He looked up at his baggage in the rack, straightened himself in his seat and felt the inner pocket where his tickets lay.

He knew very well that he still had some hours of traveling — he had made this part of the journey so often as a young man that each stage from Carcassonne toward the south was sharp and distinct in his memory — but the thought of sleep had flown out of his mind, and he continued to sit upright as the train hurried down through the growing day.

He looked forward to his homecoming, of course: he had been thinking of it with increasing pleasure for the last six months. But it would be a formidable reunion after all these years, with the whole family gathered; and still it was very early in the morning to think of the welcome at the station, the embracing, the cries of enthusiasm, the feast, without a slight tinge of melancholy. How much more agreeable it would be if he could slowly materialize at Saint-Féliu without any fuss; if by some happy dislocation of time he could already have been there for a month.

And besides the new cousins whom he certainly would not recognize, the cousins by marriage and the men and women whom he had last seen as children, there would be the births, marriages, and deaths to applaud and to deplore: and there would be this sad business of Xavier's folly to be gone into. This was the affair that most agitated the family: it had begun at least a year ago, and the storm that it had raised in Saint-Féliu had sent ripples as far as his quiet laboratory on the shores of the Luong river. He would hear it all over again, from many sources: and even those who had from the first kept him so well informed, Aunt Margot, Aunt Marinette, cousin Côme and the others, even those would certainly repeat all that they had said in their letters, would repeat it all within a very few hours of his arrival. It was inevitable; but still he would be glad to hear the latest developments, and he was willing to pay that price to hear them. A great deal could have happened during his voyage, for if Aunt Margot were right (and she was a shrewd old woman; he had a high opinion of her judgment) the whole affair was fast reaching a climax at the time he left Prabang.

There was her last letter, double-crossed in a thin, angular pattern of violet ink, most angular where it was most emphatic, and in some places illegible because of the writer's anger: it was still in his pocket, and from time to time during his voyage he had tried to decipher it.

He looked at it again, unfolding the crackling pages to the place where indignation had spread a series of hard uprights, underscored with a force that had nearly torn the paper: he hoped to surprise the meaning unawares, to catch it this time without effort. ". . . and Xavier has . . . the wretched girl . . . influence . . . *at once* . . . children . . ." Children? No. Perhaps it was "comfort";

10

though that made little difference: the whole paragraph remained obscure whatever the reading. It was frustrating to be on the edge of comprehension: but it did not matter essentially, the solution of the difficulty was at hand; and in any case, even if he could never know what the passage meant, the main lines of the affair were clear in his mind. Xavier, a middle-aged widower, the chief man of the family, the mayor and one of the most substantial inhabitants of Saint-Féliu dels Aspres, had formed a liaison with a girl young enough to be his daughter, and it appeared that there was a real danger of his marrying her.

The liaison in itself was bad enough, so public in the little town, so much on his own doorstep: the liaison was bad enough, and the early letters that had sped across the Mediterranean, the Red Sea, the Indian Ocean, and hastened across Asia to carry him the news, had been alarmed, uneasy. As cousin Côme had said, there was every opportunity for a man to have what women friends he liked in Perpignan — a separate establishment, even. It could so easily be done tactfully, and so long as the accepted gestures toward morality were made, very few people would blame him at all, even if it were quite widely known.

But in one's own village . . . It showed a cynical contempt for public opinion that could be very wounding to a man's reputation; and the family was deeply concerned with Xavier's reputation. The publicity, the local sniggering had certainly hurt them, but it was the fear for Xavier's reputation that had first sent the letters hurrying over the sea. Of course they were concerned with his good name: it was part of the general property; without it, they would all be lessened, and very much lessened; they had every right to be concerned with it. Furthermore, Xavier could never have been what he was, firmly based, solid, well connected, influential, without them, and for this reason, if for no other, he owed them consideration.

But this cause for agitation and unhappiness faded to insignificance when the far greater danger appeared: the letters redoubled in number and they grew shriller and more shrill in tone as it became more and more obvious that Xavier had lost his wits to the extent of contemplating marriage with the girl. For now it was not merely the question of property in reputation that was at stake (such reputation as Xavier could possibly retain, once it was known that he had really thought of such a crack-brained transgression): no; now the issue was that of real, tangible property, the family property, funds, land, houses. This was a common stock. It was true that it was not held communally, but it was certainly considered as a family possession: everything must be kept inside the family limits, and it was intolerable to think that Xavier, marrying, might dispose of his share like an imbecile. The letters followed hot one upon the other, and Dr. Roig, although he was so far removed in time and space and spirit, whistled gently over them, pulling his chin with that gesture that was habitual in him when he wished to express doubt, thoughtfulness, and the appreciation of a difficult situation.

He was far removed from the family. His interests had lain for so many years in another country that he could not be touched by the same immediacy, nor, even if he had been there in Saint-Féliu, would he ever have been infected by the same indignation: but still, no physical removal and no spiritual removal that he could conceive would ever take him so far away that he would remain indifferent to this fundamental danger to the family's property.

They had pressed him to come home earlier than the date he had fixed, and for a time he had been half inclined to agree: if he had thought his influence as great as Aunt

Margot so flatteringly described it — "Xavier will certainly listen to *you*. He has always had a great respect for you and for your opinion" — he might have done so. But thinking of Xavier and of their cool, superficial relationship, Dr. Roig had neither written to his cousin nor hurried his departure. A letter, indeed, on so intimate a subject, would have been impossible, especially the tirade that Aunt Margot had outlined for him: "You should say, *My dear Cousin Xavier — your conduct is unworthy of you and of our family. I blush for you, and my heart bleeds for little Dédé, whom you propose to disinherit, for the memory of Georgette, and for all our poor unjustly wounded family.*" It went on to cover two sheets of note paper. He did not suppose that Aunt Margot ever really thought that he would use this outline, although she had couched it in the shabby rhetoric that she evidently felt appropriate to a man in the act of delivering a high moral rebuke. Her own style was direct, trenchant, without literary adornment; and sometimes, when he recalled the phrases she had chosen for him, he wondered uneasily whether he had ever done anything to justify her choice; whether, unknown to himself, he had shown a tendency toward righteous pomp. He

14

hoped not. No; it was merely a release for Aunt Margot: somebody ought to thunder at Xavier in the consecrated frock-coat and shirt-front phrases, and as she dared not do it herself she had launched her bolt in an oblique direction, with a very slight hope that it might perhaps rebound and strike the intended victim. For that matter, he doubted whether Xavier had received one tenth part of the harangues that had come to him — to Alain Roig — in the form of verbatim reports, "pieces of their mind."

He smiled, too, at the old lady's heart bleeding for little Dédé. This was Xavier's son, whom he had met but recently in Haiphong, where the young man was reluctantly performing his military service. An unlikable fellow, spineless and selfish, cold; he did not think it at all probable that Aunt Margot, a clear-sighted, unsentimental woman, liked him in the least, or deceived herself into believing that she did. And as for Georgette, Xavier's wife, she had been dead these fifteen years and more. Dr. Roig could not recall any precise impression of her now: the pale, thin little personality had faded without leaving any strong trace. He remembered, with an effort, her slight, anemic form and her rather pathetic dependence on Xavier: she was not the kind of

15

woman Aunt Margot would have liked; and now that he thought about it he brought up a distinct image of Aunt Margot speaking impatiently to her — a controlled impatience with a fund of irritation behind. It was something very simple, the preservation of greengages in brandy, some trifling household operation with which Georgette could not succeed: nothing in itself, but symptomatic.

The train was running slower; its rhythm changed. The revolution of his mind slowed with that of the wheels, slower and slower, trying to keep the same rhythm, but then it was no longer possible, and he looked briskly out of the window. Here were the sidings of Narbonne, here the platform, and his face was gliding before a sea of other faces, the same height as his, and removed from his by a pane of glass and four feet of air.

The rush of people into the carriage, the anxious shouting, handing of baggage, the unscrupulous jockeying for seats, kept him tense and distracted until the train jerked on again.

The carriage settled down gradually; the passengers stared at one another, animosity died away, conversation started, and by the time they had reached the sea and had swung right-handed along the coast Dr. Roig had made out that the man and wife opposite to him were peasants, returning from a visit to their married daughter. They were describing the illness of their grandchild to the other group. "They were having the doctor, three hundred francs a visit, but the fever went on. We gave the medicines, naturally — they were paid for — but in the evening we brought the healer. He did not much care to come: he does not like to trouble himself with journeys. And then, you know, there is the jealousy with the doctors. But finally he said that as it was for *us* he would come, and when he came he held a little ball of clay over Fifine's body."

"A little ball of clay on a string."

"Special clay."

"And it showed that the blood had collected in the veins. You see? And the medicine that the doctor had been giving was to work on the nerves of the stomach. He recognized it at once by the color and the smell."

"He said that the blood must be drawn away, and he made a cataplasm with herbs from the mountain."

"Natural products. Not drugs from the pharmacy."

17

"And he said that it would draw the blood through four thicknesses of cloth."

"I was skeptical. But as it was only an external application — external, you understand? — I said 'Let us try it, at all events.' And I saw it with my own eyes: the blood came through four thicknesses of cloth. Evidently, one must believe what one sees."

"Four thicknesses. He said that four was the number for that child, as she was born in July. In the morning she was perfectly well; she had a little breakfast, just a little black coffee and some pork soup. And when the doctor came he was very pleased with her — he put it all down to his aureomycin. They say that this healer could easily be a doctor if he chose. He . . ." But the others cut her short with their own healer, a woman who trod the rheumatism out of her patients; and Dr. Roig, now that so many were shouting all at once, moved out into the corridor and stood leaning against the window.

It was very picturesque, no doubt; it was certainly a stronger and more genuine survival of folklore than local dress, songs, dances, or anything decorative; but it depressed him. He had known it all his life, of course, and when he was a child they had hung a string of garlic round his neck under his shirt. Was it connected with the general lack of religious faith? The necessity for something magic? Some day he would ask a colleague whether these pests were as frequent in the believing parts — Brittany, for example, or in the north where the Catholic trades unions were strong.

They were passing along the edge of one of the great salt lagoons now: a flight of avocets, black and white against the pale water, distracted him from his thoughts on popular medicine, and his mind went back to Saint-Féliu and cousin Xavier.

The girl was the daughter of the grocer in the rue Joffre. Madeleine. He knew the parents, Jean Fajal and Dominique, and he knew the shop, a little cavern under the arcades with a grove of dried sausage and stockfish and candles hanging from its ceiling, and dark butts of wine disappearing into the shadows on either hand; not very prosperous, but always full of black old women gossiping, and with Fajal's two vineyards and the market garden it would be enough to keep them comfortably. But he could not remember any daughter. Obviously, she would have been a child when last he was home; and there were so many children, all alike except to their parents.

A child of about twelve or thirteen she must have been: he tried to picture the shop with a child in it, but that brought him nothing, and he ran the closer relations of the Fajals through his mind to see if he could fix the child in another surrounding. There was Fajal's sister almost next door, in the mercery, and lower down on the corner there was the other sister at the tobacco shop. Was it that extraordinary, ethereal child, the one he had seen at the tobacconist's? He remembered how he had stared; a slim child (though at first he had not known she was a child — she had no age, neither young nor old for the first moment of that encounter) with ash-blond hair and a perfect, exquisite face and pale eyes. No. That girl's name was Carmen, and she had died — meningitis — after he had left. This Madeleine would be her cousin. If she looked anything like her, no wonder Xavier behaved strangely. Though in all likelihood if Carmen had grown up she would have coarsened like the other girls: that strange remoteness would have come heavily to earth with adolescence; and the inevitable growth of body, atrophy of mind, the invasion of clothes, make-up, frizzled hair, would all have buried that lovely child deeper than ever the earth did now.

Still he could not see any little girl called Madeleine Fajal, or rather Pou-naou — for although the family's name was Fajal on letters and documents, nobody in Saint-Féliu called them anything but Pou-naou, from the circumstance of Jean Fajal's father having owned the house by the new fountain, or pump. Jean Pou-naou, Thérèse Pou-naou, Mimi Pou-naou who married the son of René l'Empereur: but Jean's uncle, old Pou-naou's brother, was called Ferrand because he was a smith, and all his branch of the family were Ferrands too. And this diversity of names ran through the town, the interrelated, closely knit, cross-knit town of cousins and remoter kin, to the utter confusion of strangers, and to their exclusion. None but a native, born to it and growing up with it, could hold it all in his head: but Alain Roig had absorbed it in his youngest days, and although the years between had carried away so much, that remained, surprisingly complete and ready to his hand. Without searching at all he remembered that Mimi Pou-naou had married Louis l'Empereur, the son of René l'Empereur — the old soldier of Cochin-China who nominally owned the tobacco shop that Mimi ran while her husband went to sea after the sardines and anchovies — and that René l'Empereur, who was officially called René Prats, had received his name very early, when Napoleon III had dandled him for a moment, thus changing the family surname, which for generations had been Pitg-a-fangc, Wade in the muck, from an origin too gross to record.

So although he could not remember the child Madeleine as a person, he could fix her exactly in her place, surround her with her relations and her contemporaries. He could define her, like a geometrical locus, in relation to a number of determined entities, a very large number in this case. Still, it was irritating not to be able to manage his memory better: he had often heard about the girl, and that should have perpetuated a visual image. Heard about her, that is, before all this fuss; for she had been something of a protégée of his Aunt Margot. He had heard about her accompanying Aunt Margot to Perpignan to see a parade, helping with Aunt Margot's orphans: "I made the rest of the silk you sent me into a collar and cuffs for Madeleine." But particularly he had heard about her when she married one Francisco Cortade: it was a marriage very much disapproved by Aunt Margot and by all the girl's family — a most unequal match, by all that he heard. It had made Aunt Margot angry to see Madeleine, an educated girl, able to speak correct French and to present herself anywhere, capable of holding a serious position (she could type), throwing herself away in marriage to a young fisherman with nothing at all, a young man furthermore who was said to be idle and to have absurd pretensions. She had been angry, too, because she felt that Madeleine had been deceitful; she had never told Aunt Margot the full state of her feelings, and the marriage had come as a disagreeable surprise. She had been so angry, indeed, that she had not fully restored the girl to favor until the marriage ended in disaster. Dr. Roig had heard about this: the young man had apparently run away with a film star — an event for Saint-Féliu — and Madeleine, having taken her desertion very hard, had been comforted and sustained by Aunt Margot.

Now it cannot have been so very long after that, he reflected, arranging the chronology of events in his mind, that I had that letter from cousin Côme with the facetious reference to Xavier making his typist work overtime: that was the beginning. Though perhaps in fact it was not the true beginning, for cousin Côme had an obscene mind and he could not see a man and a woman together without being sure that they coupled furtively, that they had a guilty relationship

— a state of affairs that was in itself intrinsically amusing, very funny indeed to Côme.

Perpignan. In the fury of the arrival Dr. Roig slipped back into his corner seat, where he could keep safely out of reach of the contending parties, the strong body of those who wished to get out, and the still stronger body of those who were going to get on at any cost at all. With each stop in its southward journey the train had met a more determined set of boarders (with each kilometer the fiery rudeness of the people grew) and here, almost at its last halt before the Spanish frontier, almost at the extremity of France, it was received by a horde so fierce that it might have been fleeing from the plague, or a devouring fire behind. By this alone he could have told that he was in his own country, but now all the voices were Catalan too, for further proof; and that familiar harshness stirred him as no harmonious tongue could ever have done. It was not a beautiful language, he was bound to admit, and the people who were speaking it were neither decorative nor well-mannered; but it was his own language, this was his native country, and these were his own people.

The compartment was crowded, and he could distinguish the accents of Elne in the plain, of the mountain villages, and of his own Catalans of the sea: the man whose elbow was sticking so painfully into his side was certainly from Banyuls, by the way he had of speaking. He gathered that the grapes were doing quite well, and that if nothing went wrong for the next two or three weeks they would be beginning the vendanges in the plain; that the price of apricots and peaches had been so low that it had barely been worth picking them; that the price of everything was going up and up; and that the youth of today was worthless.

The well-known phrases came out again with a predictability that was charming for a returning exile: the conversation was like a familiar childish tune on a musical box; it might prove maddening in time, but after a long interval it could be heard again with affection and delight.

"They are all bandits. All of them, Communists, Socialists, Radical-Socialists, MRP and Gaullistes: all bandits. Every one is in it for what he can get out of it, and the country can go to the devil."

"They do nothing to protect their own people. It is not worth selling our wine at the market price; our early vegetables and fruit rot on the ground, and all the time ships are arriving at Sète and Port-Vendres loaded down with wine from North Africa and fruit from Italy. Someone says to a minister 'Té, here is a million francs: I want a license to import a hundred tons of peaches' and it is done. It is as simple as that, and meanwhile we starve," said the fat man.

"I never vote for any of them."

"They are all bandits."

"When I was young the father of a family had some authority. At dawn he showed his son a mattock and said 'To the vineyard.' And to the vineyard the boy would go. He would take a loaf and a skin of wine and an onion and work there until dark. Now what does he do?"

The train was running fast now, lickety-lick across the plain, the plain with its drilled armies of peach trees, almonds, and apricots stretching away in interminable files: a hundred times a minute a perspective opened, a straight lane of precise trees with a green stream of garden-stuff running down between; the perspective opened, slanting rapidly to the full, held there for an instant, slanted fast away and was gone as the next began to open; and between each pair there was a fragmentary hint of diagonals, opened and closed so quickly that nothing could be distinguished but a sense of ordered space. Most of the peaches were picked already, but still there were a few late orchards with the fruit glowing among the leaves, peaches that looked too big for the trees: they would be the big dorats, he thought, and the word brought the memory of that wonderful bitter-sweet prussic-acid taste and the smell of the downy skin.

They passed Corneilla del Vercol, and he had hardly said to himself "Now we begin to turn" when he felt the beginning of the centrifugal pressure, his weight pressing outward against the side, as the train ran fast on to the long curve down to the sea, and the Canigou came into sight, sharp and clear in the morning sky, still the morning sky, for it was hardly more than breakfast-time. There was a belt of cloud lying across the middle height, but the three tall peaks stabbed up hard and dominating. It was the mountain that ruled the plain; and the plain seen without the mountain was nothing but a dull stretch of intensely cultivated land instead of a preparation and the foreground for a magnificent piece of set scenery: a little obvious and romantic, perhaps, but superb in its kind, composed on the very grandest scale, and instantly, overwhelming effective.

The long curve went on: the Canigou moved imperceptibly into the middle of the window, and now by leaning against the glass and peering forward he could see the long curtain of the Pyrenees, dark, with the sun behind them. That was the limit of the plain, the wall of dark mountains that ran headlong to the sea, and that was his own piece of the world, there where the sea and the mountains joined.

It was very near now. On the skyline he could see the towers, high up, remote against the sky, the ancient solitary towers against the Algerine rovers, the Moors who had sacked the coast for so many hundred years; they stood one behind the other, far spaced, to carry the alarm like beacons: they were his final landmarks. The train bore away and away to the left, running directly now for the edge of the sea, for there was no way through the mountains, and even at the very rim of the land it was tunnel and cutting, cutting and tunnel all the way, to get along at all.

The round towers, remote and deserted on the high bare peaks, had always been the symbols of homecoming for him, for he had been able to see them from his bedroom window as a boy, and for ever after, when he came back from school or from the university or (as he did now) from foreign parts, it always appeared to him that this was the last of the last steps, for looking up to those far towers his line of sight could be reflected

28

down, through his own window, back into his bedroom.

They had crossed the river, and the richest of the plain was left behind: there were trees and rectangles of market-garden still, but they were islands in the blue-green sea of vines. An ocean of vines, that would make your heart ache to think of the picking of all the grapes. He got up, worked through the legs and the crossing lines of talk and stood in the corridor to watch for the first arrival of the sea on the other side.

Already the plain was finished. They were running through the first hills, the hills that started with such abrupt determination, instantly changing the very nature of the countryside. Now the sandy cuttings were crowned with agaves, some with their flower-spikes thrust twenty feet above, and the sides of the railway were covered with prickly pear, starting out of an acid, bitter-looking soil. And here the round sides of the hills were cut and cut with terraces, terraces everywhere, and on the terraces vineyards, olives, vineyards, cork oaks, pines and more vineyards, vineyards on slopes where a man could hardly stand to work them. Then suddenly there it was, the sea blue and faintly lapping in a little deep-cut bay. A tunnel cut off all light, and he stood in the eddying smoke, suspended: through the tunnel, and there it was again; the same bay, one would have said — it had the same reddish cliffs dropping down to the bright shingle and the waveless sea; but it was not the same, for here on the right was a grove of cork oaks with crimson trunks. Tunnel again, and the bay repeated. Here the difference was a boat drawn up, a bright blue boat with the strange crucifix of a lateen mast and yard.

They passed by Collioure, with its ghastly new hotels and its seething mass of tourists: it had been such a charming little town, he thought sadly, as he peered round the bulk of the latest hotel at the tiny beach where men and women lay tight-packed on the dirty stones and overlapping into the water where a thousand stewed together in the tideless wash. Sad, sad: he thanked God that Saint-Féliu had no clock tower to be painted, no beach for bathing, no drains, no hotel, and hardly a bath at all in the whole town. And no Beaux-Arts to protect it, he added, catching the trite cynicism of the people in his compartment. Collioure, Port-Vendres, Banyuls, Puig del Mas. Now the line was a little farther from the sea, and higher up. The road ran with it, and there was a green bus, racing along to keep up with the train, passengers waving madly, and a faint shrieking audible above the thunder of the rails. At the turn he would catch a glimpse of Saint-Féliu: he opened the window and leaned out, screwing his eyes tight against the wind: there, exactly where his mind had placed it, there it was, a tight, rose-pink swarm of roofs, packed tight within the round gray walls, pressed in by the hills, a full, broad crescent that rose in steep tiers from the pure curve of the bay; and between the seaward wall and the sea, the arc of fishing boats drawn up.

He had just that moment to receive it all, and then the wall of the cutting whipped between. Here was old Bisau's orange grove; green bronze the oranges. Next would come the brake of tall bamboos, and then the tunnel. He was back in the carriage, standing at his seat to lower his baggage. The train screamed for the tunnel, roared in, and the light was gone. He stood there, swaying in the darkness. When the light came back he would be home.

Chapter Two

When Madeleine was a little girl she was a plain creature, and timid. Her form was the undistinguished, pudgy, shapeless form of most children; there was no feminine delicacy in her face — or very little — and if her hair had been cut short she might have passed for a plain little boy.

Nobody considered her a good-looking child; and even her mother and her aunts, when they had finished scrubbing and frizzing and ornamenting her for her first Communion, could say no more than that the little Baixas girl (a downright ugly one) did not look half so attractive. Madeleine felt the lack of conviction in their voices, and she agreed with them entirely; but for her part she did not mind at all. Indeed, she laughed heartily when her father said what a good thing it was that she had a veil; for in her own family, in the dark room behind the cave-like shop, or in the clear, white, dustless mercery next door, she was a cheerful soul, happy to find humor in the thinnest joke, and brimming over with that *élan* which caused her to talk, chant, and spin about for the greater part of the day. It was only when she was out of her home that shyness came down over her: then she would blush if a stranger spoke to her, and in an unfamiliar house she had no voice at all.

She was plain and timid, then, and even in her own opinion devoid of charm or importance; but this did not prevent her from pursuing Francisco Cortade, her schoolfellow. She pursued him openly, without disguise, and he accepted her attentions, if not with pleasure, at least without repulsion.

She thought he was the most beautiful creature she had ever seen; and without exaggeration he was a lovely little boy — huge eyes, a great deal of black and curling hair, and an absurd complexion. She brought him presents from the shop, rousquilles — the little round dry white-iced cakes the Catalans eat on holidays — twigs of raw licorice from the mountains, nuts, anything that could be concealed under her pinafore; and if she could not bring him anything from the shop she would give him the croissant or the fougasse that she was supposed to eat at eleven. It was a disinterested passion, for although he would take her offerings civilly enough, he would hardly ever let her play with him — he was too old, far too old, he said — and if he ever let her walk with him from school he would desert her instantly for a troop of boys. He treated her very badly, but it seemed just to her, and she was grateful for his kindness in always taking what she brought.

Then occasionally he would be very kind: on Thursdays or in the holidays she would sometimes find him by the boat his father fished in, the red and yellow *Amphitrite*; and then, if he were alone, he would let her come aboard and be the crew or the enemy, or whatever fitted in.

It was some time after her first Communion that the first hint of modesty showed itself in Madeleine. Up until that time she would reply "He has just run away," or "He is down by the sea" to the question "Where is your sweetheart?" — a question that the people of the street would ask her once or twice a day. Now she would frown heavily and deny him, or she would say that she did not know where he was, and did not care: and now she stopped bringing him rousquilles, and in doing so she saved her conscience many a reproach and her heart many a wild fluttering. It was not that she stole the rousquilles or the licorice, but she took them without explicit leave: she had always felt that there was a great difference, but still she always chose the time when there was nobody in the shop, and more than once, caught standing on a chair beneath the rousquilles' shelf, or spoken to when the offering was half hidden in her pinafore, she had gone pale with horror, or scarlet red; and afterward it needed a fair amount of argument to convince herself that she had done no wrong. But now this almost daily trial was done, and now at eleven o'clock she ate her roll or cake, and she ate it skipping or howling with the other little girls.

At first Francisco did not notice this change, but after some days it was borne in upon him that he no longer had a devoted follower, and that the stream of rousquilles had dried up, apparently for ever. He was puzzled, worried, at a loss to understand. He could not say how it had happened, nor when it had begun: and then there was no reason; he had not been unkind to her for weeks. After some thought he began to make advances. He left the school quickly and lurked about until she appeared, but when he said that she could walk with him if she liked, she ran fast away to go hand in hand with Carmen and Denise, and he was left sad and foolish behind.

Two days later he bought two croissants

and gave her one at break: he waited until she had finished her own before he offered it, and she was glad to take it. In an access of reconciliation he said that he had a dried sea horse for her in the boat, and they shared his second croissant.

It is true that he soon recovered the upper hand, but it was a more even friendship now, and so it continued. In the village school of Saint-Féliu such things could be; elsewhere they might have been mocked and laughed to scorn, but not here. They continued, consecrated now by habit, rising form after form, reaching decimals and long division; they learned the Merovingian kings and passed the gap-toothed stage; by the time they reached the Revolution Francisco was already talking gruff.

It was toward this time that Dominique, Madeleine's mother, began to look pensive when she saw the two walk down the narrow street together. For a long, long while Madeleine and her sweetheart had been a joke with the street, and Dominique had laughed as much as any. She had called her daughter a hussy, a one for the men, and so on: she had often and often called Francisco into the shop to give him his pick of the squashed peaches, or a caramel or a piece of gingerbread. She was a fat, jolly woman in those days, and she liked to see children pleased and happy around her. In this she was in no way exceptional, in Saint-Féliu or anywhere else, but she was exceptional for Saint-Féliu in that she succeeded — succeeded, that is, in making them pleased and happy when they were with her. It was not that she was clever — far from that. She was rather a stupid woman, and given to long spells of absence, during which she would stare in front of her like a glazed cow, thinking of nothing at all; but by some gift of being she was better at the management of a child than any woman in the quarter. It may have been her plumpness, for fat people are said to be calm of spirit, or it may have been some natural sweetness, but whatever the cause, the house never knew those screaming, tearing scenes that broke out three or four times a day somewhere along the street, those horribly commonplace rows in which a woman, dark with hatred and anger, may be seen dragging a child by the arm, flailing at its head, and screaming, screaming, screaming a great piercing flood of abuse, sarcasm, and loathing right into its convulsed and wretched little face. These scenes were so ordinary in Saint-Féliu that anyone turning to stare would be known at once for a foreigner.

It was not that these things shocked Dominique. And it is possible that the rare foreigner who did stop in dismay made too much of them: after all, the town had been brought up that way, and every mother in her time had been alternately slapped and kissed, spoiled and cowed. Everything was covered by the expression "It is stronger than me," delivered with a little self-satisfied smirk, or "It makes my hand itch." No further excuse to public opinion was necessary, and none to themselves: and in fact, though the children screamed, and though some of them grew up rather queer, not many died of their raising. On the other hand, outsiders could say, and say truly, that whereas in some foreign countries parricide is a monstrous crime, scarcely appearing once or twice in a hundred years, a thing to be spoken of with horror, remembered and shuddered upon for generations, yet here, in the local paper, it would not be worth a banner headline: a parricide would be found on an inner page, squeezed between the daily recipe and a piece on the control of insect pests.

Dominique could not be shocked by what she had seen for all her life — could not react from the normal — but she was exceptional, and she remained exceptional. She did not batter her little girl about, she did not pull her hair, she did not slap her legs and shriek abuse at her — her voice did not even possess the bitter scolding note of the daily shrew. This was something so rare that it would have earned her the dislike of the street (no people are quicker to resent an implied criticism) if it had not been for the fact that Madeleine was, in general, somewhat less irritating than the other children: therefore, of course, there was no virtue in Dominique's not beating her. Not that Madeleine was what could by any distortion of the term be called a good child, whatever the neighbors might say: she was dirty (when she was a little girl), untruthful, and dishonest. But being less battered, she was less dirty, untruthful, and dishonest than the rest. Certainly she was less irritating, for not only was she endowed with a happy, affectionate nature, but also with a mother who was protected from the smaller vexations of the world by well-ordered nerves and a high degree of mental calm: for in the matter of irritation, it is essential that there should be two people present; the worst-bred ape of a child cannot be irritating alone in a howling wilderness, and Madeleine, even at her worst, could not provoke a mother removed by a boundless expanse of absence, sitting at her counter or leaning on it, with her eyes round, wide open, and fixed upon nothing, nothing whatever.

But still, kind though Dominique was, her kindness recognized a vast difference between those who belonged to her family and those who did not; and now that Madeleine was growing older — old enough now that no one could possibly mistake her for a boy — she looked at Francisco, and wished that her daughter had chosen some other man's son to appropriate.

The thought was no sooner clear in her mind than she spoke it: this was her way, and unless she were in one of her moods of abstraction it was rare that she let out a breath without some words upon it. It was her comfort to talk: the greater part of her life was passed in a haze of words, and if she had been prevented from talking with her customers, with her neighbors if there were nobody in the shop, or with herself if she were kept in alone by her duties, if she had been cut off from that delight, she would have pined clean away. Without her little gossip, she owned, she would never get through her day; and the life of a small shopkeeper in Saint-Féliu was no slight affair: she was up before it was light in the winter to meet the lorry that brought the milk, and already there would be customers waiting; then from that time she would not shut the door until ten o'clock on an early evening or eleven on a late one. This she did seven days a week for the whole year round. In some manner, too, between opening and closing the door, she fed her family and did her housework, besides selling salt cod, chick-peas, haricots, chicory, wreaths of garlic, bowls, glasses, soap, oil, wine, cheese, peaches, apricots, persimmons, melons, figs, medlars, all the fruit of their garden, all their vegetables, and brooms, sulphur candles, votive candles, ordinary candles, and a hundred other things beyond the list. This was in addition to collecting, arranging, and weighing every scrap of information about the private lives of all the families in the town, collating it with former knowledge and passing it on in a better form.

She had a little help from her husband in the evenings with the accounts, but he worked nearly as many hours as she did, with the market-garden, the two vineyards, and the insurance-collecting that kept him so much from home, and she could be said to run the shop singlehanded. There was, of course, her sister-in-law next door, who had not half the custom, nor a quarter, and who would spend the most part of her day as often as not in measuring out the rice or sugar, or in preparing the lunch while Dominique satisfied the customers. There was also Mimi from the tobacco shop down on the corner of the street; when her husband was not at sea she would leave the shop in his charge and come to help at the busy time of day, for the shop, Dominique's shop, was the ancestral place of trade, and they all felt a particular loyalty toward it.

But this is not directly concerned with her thought about Francisco. The only person in the shop at the time of Dominique's thought was an old woman who came down from Ayguafret in the mountains and carried back her provisions in a donkey cart.

"It will be all right when he goes away for his military service," said Dominique.

The old woman was deaf; she replied that she would have no honey that year. The bees were all dying.

"When he goes away for his military service it will be all right," repeated Dominique, in a stronger voice.

"Who?"

"Francisco."

"Whose Francisco?"

"En Jaume Camairerrou's Francisco."

"I never heard of him."

"Yes, you have. He is En Cisoul's cousin: your own godchild's cousin-german."

"Which En Cisoul?"

"The faubourg En Cisoul, of course," adding in a louder voice, "En Jourda's son, your own godchild."

"Oh? Well, I don't mind him."

"I say it will be all right when he has gone for his military service."

"I dare say: but it was five francs a kilo in the war."

It was from that time on that Madeleine began to feel that her family did not like Francisco. It was not that they forbade her to play with him — nothing so hard or definite — but there was an air of disapproval, and a determination not to be pleased with Francisco that survived even the nine days' wonder of his name being in the paper: he was first in a drawing competition for all the primary schools of the department. Jean Fajal, a remote and silent man, usually benign, though wordless, stared at the paper for a long while and said, "He will grow proud, no doubt: too proud for his trade."

They had every worldly reason for discouraging the association. Francisco came from the most savage part of the faubourg, el Cagareill, the quarter in front of the sea, and his father, Jaume Cortade, called Camairerrou, was as poor as he was savage. He was very savage. Francisco himself was the product of a freakish passion for a Genoese woman, a strange waif who came in with one of the Corsican fishing boats: Camairerrou installed her in his uncouth hovel, where she died among the nets and lobster pots within the year.

But it went on, in spite of their disapproval: it went on, but of necessity they saw less of one another once school was over and done with. Francisco went first, being the older: the schoolmaster wanted him to stay and go on to the school at Argelès, said it was a waste to leave now, and even called on old Camairerrou; but it was no good, Francisco wanted to be out, and the old man could see no reason why a boy who could pull on a rope should stay penned in a school. So he left, and at once he was a man. On the last day of his last term he was a boy, playing quite childishly with the other boys in the street as they went home; and on the first day of the new term he passed them as they straggled by the fish-market, he passed them with his sea-boots on, carrying a basket with En Cisoul, a hundredweight of sardines, for the boats had been out all night. He nodded to them

44

as he went by, but it was a man nodding to boys of his acquaintance, not a boy grinning at his equals.

This change impressed Madeleine beyond words: she had always thought him wonderful, but this new fine creature in tall sea-boots and a scarlet handkerchief struck her dumb: she felt that she had been far too familiar, far too presuming, and for a while she fell back into her position of an unarmed, suppliant admirer.

But she too was changing. She was not yet the equal of her lovely cousin, Mimi's daughter Carmen, but her childish plainness had quite gone. She was growing into her features, and she was shooting up like a young willow; already she had that supple, upright, thoroughbred carriage that is supposed to come from carrying burdens on one's head. Her nose was still unformed, and a great deal of the child lingered about her face, but her fantastic bloom of complexion had begun, and it was obvious, even to her family, that she was growing into a very handsome young woman.

It was at this time that she attracted the attention of Mme. Roig. Mme. Roig had known her before — she knew everybody — but she had not taken any particular notice of the girl until one day Madeleine and her

Aunt Mimi decorated the chapel of the Curé d'Ars, acting as substitutes for three women who had all eaten the same poisoned dish of mussels. Mme. Roig was a widow, the widow of Gaston Roig, of the rich family of Saint-Féliu: she was a great power in the parish church, a childless woman, respected, but rather feared than liked in the village. She invited Madeleine to her house, interested herself in her, and interfered with her natural development.

It appeared at first that Mme. Roig had probably taken her up with a view to converting her, for Madeleine was a Protestant — a Protestant at least in the mild and unemphatic manner of the Protestants of Saint-Féliu. So was her family, except for Mimi l'Empereur, but there was no sectarian fire in their religion, none in Saint-Féliu at all, where every day, from ten o'clock to half past ten, the curé and the pasteur walked together on the beach. This was a strange anomaly in such a vivid place, with violence and passion overflowing for the smallest disagreeing word: but there it was, a settled and acknowledged fact. Perhaps the explanation was that the people had almost no religious sense at all, were almost wholly pagan in their lives: but whatever was the underlying cause, they seemed as happy in the temple as the church, and practically indifferent to both.

But if it was conversion, Mme. Roig did not persist: she was content to have the child, the young woman one might almost say, as a very pretty and submissive friend, overflowing with vitality and cheerfulness, a companion for odd afternoons. Presently Mme. Roig found that Madeleine had grown quite indispensable to her: she had a great deal to do, looking after her own big house and her nephew's too, as well as keeping a strict eye on the curé's house-keeper. She had a great deal to do, being a thorough, active-minded woman: there were her orphans, her charities, the decoration and the cleaning of the church, the dressing of the saints, and she found a younger pair of legs very useful. It was not only this severely practical view, however, that made Mme. Roig feel that it would be impossible to do without her: when the worst of Madeleine's shyness had worn off — those early visits had been hours of torment for her, torment in anticipation chiefly, for she always enjoyed it when she had been there a little while — when she became more confident with Mme. Roig, she entered wonderfully into the old lady's somewhat dried affections.

In the end Mme. Roig justified herself by giving Madeleine presents from time to time, suitable presents like woolen stockings and calico drawers, and sometimes lace and handkerchiefs; by a private determination to do something handsome when Madeleine should marry; and by teaching her to sew, to keep accounts, and type. Mme. Roig could sew and sum admirably well herself; she had learned the first in a convent that was as famous for its sewing, its embroidery and lace as for its piety — a convent in the north of France — and the second while she looked after her brother's house, he being vicaire général at Perpignan. But the typewriter, as she admitted, was beyond her competence; however, she did not condemn it for that reason or its novelty. She thought it a more useful accomplishment than the piano, and she bought a M. Boileau's system of typewriting and taught Madeleine from it on the machine in her nephew's office — taught her much as a man who cannot swim instructs his pupils from the edge of the swimming-bath.

Madeleine and Francisco, then, were very much more apart than they had been for years; but still it was rare that a day went by without their meeting. All through the long summer the boats were out almost every

48

night, and Madeleine, hitherto a slugabed, would be up and waiting at the crack of dawn, standing at the edge of the sea, watching for the boats to come round the point. They would come in, nearly always from the north, round the short breakwater on the left-hand horn of the little bay's crescent, and if the tramontane was blowing, as it was so often, the first would come in fast, heeling from the wind and shaving the steep-to foot of the jetty, and the crew would all cheer as they came round it. There would be a man standing in the bows, leaning up along the tall prow-piece and outlined black against the dun sail, and the moment he saw the beach he would utter the long, wavering hail of the first boat in, the ritual cry of Blue Fish. Then the buyers on the shingle would shriek back in their strange trade jargon, and before the long boat crunched up against the shore the sardines would be sold.

Sometimes it was Francisco's boat that was first, but not often, for it was not a lucky boat: if any of the boats of Saint-Féliu caught a dolphin or a shark or a moonfish or any of those unwanted captures that rip the sardine and anchovy nets to fragments, it was the *Amphitrite*: sometimes, and not rarely, the *Amphitrite* would be the last of the boats to come in, to reach a shore deserted by the buyers, nobody on it at all but the remaining fishermen of the more fortunate crews and Madeleine.

But whether it came early or late it looked beautiful to Madeleine, the long, low boat like a greyhound, with its queer, squat, forward-raked mast — a strange, urgent angle for a mast — its tapering yard with the great triangle of a sail, and the crew crowded all along the length of the low gunwale.

They did not speak now on the beach: a catching of the eye and a private smile was all, now that they were so much more conscious. It was not the same in the evening, however; the atmosphere was different then, and when there was dancing on the Place they always danced together. Charming they looked, charming, as they skipped busily round and round in the Saint-Féliu version of a quickstep, and more charming by far when they stood hand in hand, grave and poised, in the entranced circle of the sardana dancers, with the harsh Catalan pipes screaming through the summer darkness, and the faint brush-brush of all the feet, rope-soled, cutting fast to the measure of the drum, while the hands and heads, held high, swam as if they were hung upon the music.

In the evenings, too, they walked together, aimlessly among shadows on the ramparts, or on to the jetty, where the warm stone gave back the heat of the long day's sun. They would stay until it was time for Francisco to go and help prepare the boat for the sea: often they would stay longer, and each would have hard reproach that made no impression upon their closed and dreaming faces.

Now the first hint of the everlasting shrew began to show in Dominique's voice, and now it grew still more confirmed in Thérèse. They would set upon Madeleine when she returned, in turn or both together.

"Where have you been?"

"Yes. Where have you been?"

"She has been with that good-for-nothing"

"Starveling"

"Do-nought"

"Lover of hers."

"For shame, Madeleine."

"Madeleine, for shame."

"You knew there was so much to do in the shop."

"You should help your mother in the evenings."

"Not run about like a bitch in heat."

"Or a cat in the night."

"With her legs swollen by standing all day."

"When I was a girl I helped my mother."

"We all helped our mother, poor thing."

"Poor little thing, alas."

They both shed tears, and began again, "Carmen helps her mother."

"Yes, Carmen does not roam about."

"Carmen is a good girl."

"If Mme. Roig knew she would have nothing more to do with you."

"She would say, 'Madeleine, my heart bleeds for your mother and aunts, poor things.' "

"And that would be an end of your fine goings-on."

Madeleine heard little of it all, and they hardly expected that she would listen attentively; but sometimes her complacent air, like a cat that has eaten the cream, so provoked them that her aunt, rushing round the cloth-covered table with the lamp on it, would shake her frantically by the shoulders, shouting in her ear "Now then; now, now!"

Her mother never shook her, but she nodded when Thérèse did, and when the man of the house was there during one of these scoldings she would say, "It is only your father's goodness of heart that prevents him from beating you," in a voice directed as much at Jean as at Madeleine.

Dominique was becoming seriously worried now, and she longed for the time when the young fellow should be taken away for his military service, far away, to the other end of the world for preference, and for a long, long time. But although Francisco grew taller every day, and looked more and more like a full-grown man, capable of any mischief — Dominique's clients already assured her that he was better at making Sunday-children than catching fish — his class was still far from being called. And daily, as he grew, he appeared more and more undesirable in her eyes. He had already earned a bad reputation among the fishermen as a lazy fellow, a passenger, and if the crew of the *Amphitrite* had not been afraid of old Camairerrou, Francisco would have been on the beach after a few weeks' trial. They did not like him. It was not merely that he was backward in hauling on the nets, waiting to be told what to do instead of being there in front of the word like another boy; it was not that when it came to picking up the great skeins of sun-dried nets at midday Francisco was not to be found; it was not merely the usual complaints against idleness and inefficiency; it was worse than that. He brought them bad luck. There was no doubt that some man or some thing did. The season's fishing, the long, long hours of night at sea, the wet cold, the interminable pulling on the heavy sweeps when a dead calm fell, all the hardships they had undergone, did not bring them in enough to live the winter through. Not enough, that is, for the married men: old savages like Camairerrou or El Turrut would hibernate, staying in bed for days on end with three loaves and a jug of wine, emerging from time to time to fish from the shore with a rod or to indulge in a night's smuggling over the border. The others, once they had looked to their vineyards, would have to find work, either day-laboring or as stevedores at Port-Vendres when the Spanish schooners came up with oranges.

Somebody had brought them bad luck; for nearly all the other boats had made enough for the whole year round, and their crews would spend the winter repairing their gear, pottering about with a calking-iron and a pot of paint, preparing for the spring: somebody had brought them bad luck, and it was certainly Francisco. Not only was he unhandy and awkward, the sort of person who smelt of bad luck, but once he had hurried on board, hot from the firemen's ball, still prinked out in collar and tie, and *wearing shoes*. In a gloomy silence they had thrown them into the sea: but what was that feeble act against such an omen? How much could a pair of shoes propitiate? Very little: and bad was all their fishing, very bad.

The autumns, then, took Francisco away; but they did not take him far, only along the coast to Port-Vendres one year, and to Collioure another. There he made friends with a Swedish painter and came home with a box of colors and a parcel of brushes, filled with enthusiasm for the new way of painting. He had never given up drawing or painting little water colors since he left school, and now that he showed himself in Saint-Féliu with easel and canvas in the grand manner the people took it very calmly. They did not think much of his new way of painting; they had never thought much of his former manner — painstaking representation — for he had never had the trick of taking likenesses, which alone they admired; but they tolerated him. There are countries where it would not be permissible for a young fisherman to take up his stand and paint a street in public; the youths of his own age would not allow it for a moment, the little boys would stone him and even the dogs would be outraged; but France is not one of them. Saint-Féliu was quite prepared to watch Francisco paint, so long as he did not give himself airs.

What little stir it did create tended to put Francisco into a slightly romantic rather than a ridiculous position, and this vexed Dominique, vexed and worried her. But if she had been able to hear the conversation of the two young people in the fragrant dusk of the orange grove beyond the tunnel she would have worried less. The conversation now took the form of a lecture upon aesthetics, very earnest, and very long: listening, Dominique would have heard nothing but Francisco's voice going on and on, grave and expositive, sometimes deriding and sometimes indignant, but never pausing, except for the moments when Madeleine said yes. Dominique would have heard some strange things indeed, that a picture should never tell a story, that it need not even show a known form; that the cave men painted finer things than Ingres, and that it was very wicked to be an academic. She would have heard the words impressionist, primitive, futurist, expressionist, and abstract recurring again and again; and again and again the litany of Picasso, Braque, and Matisse, Maillol, Dufy, and Vlaminck. She would have heard all that and much more, if she had had the patience; but she would have heard nothing to cause her alarm. Dominique need not have worried, but she did, and the more she did so, the more eagerly she looked forward to Francisco's calling-up: all safety seemed to lie in that blessed event. In her own short bloom she had been a flighty piece, widely affectionate, and she was sure that it would be the same with Madeleine: a few months' absence and the young man would be lost.

But still the years passed slowly, and still he did not go. She did have one respite, for Carmen died, and at the tail of her noisy grief the recollection came to her that now Madeleine was to be secluded and dressed in black. This dried her tears, and the event that she had sincerely mourned seemed now a positive relief.

Yet even in Saint-Féliu mourning for a cousin cannot last for ever: it can take up a great deal of energy, black cloth, and time, but it has an end, and the day came when Dominique and her two sisters sat working out the date again, the time of the young man's removal, reckoning up the months with an angry impatience.

As it came nearer Dominique looked forward to it with pleasure and relief: but when it came she was not in Saint-Féliu, nor was Madeleine, nor was her husband, nor any one of her uncounted relatives and friends and customers. Grass, knee-high, was growing against her shuttered door, and between the cobbles of the street grass and long-drawn weeds strained up toward the narrow slit of sky: the fishing boats, dragged up to the Place and chained there, lay sunk in a green haze of grass, and in the grass the trodden lanes showed the track of the German sentry's round.

The inhabitants of Saint-Féliu were dispersed about the interior, and the Fajals were far inland, right under the mountains of Andorra, where some remote cousins had a farm. Francisco, with many others, was in Germany, working at forced labor in a factory; a great many more were in camps as prisoners of war; a few were in North Africa, having escaped through Spain; and six from Saint-Féliu were dead, killed in the early fighting.

It was a strange, slow nightmare, all that period, impossible to relate to real life. That only began again with the return to Saint-Féliu, with the opening of the long-shut familiar doors, with the re-creation of something like the known old life, going to the same pump with the same crazy, shrieking

58

handle, going up the same number of stairs to bed, waking in the dark to hear the same cry of the fishermen waking the laggards, "Xica-té, es l'alba."

Real life appeared to begin again as soon as the Germans had gone, but in fact a long interval of excess came between that time and the new normality — excess of happiness, excess of relief, excess in eating. It would be wrong to add excess in welcoming the return of the men from captivity; excess is not the word at all, but rather unbounded rejoicing and a tendency in the free and overflowing generosity of that time to attribute equal worth to all who returned from that gray and brutish land. Thus Francisco and the others who had gone with him were received with almost as much joy as the soldiers whose glory was reflected on them. It was not that they did not deserve a hearty welcome from their friends, but these young men who had been taken for forced labor had done nothing heroic: they had not volunteered to go, it is true, but they had let themselves be seized, while others had taken to the mountains rather than work for the enemy, and some had gone over the seas to fight again. At the time Madeleine had wondered; even in the middle of her sorrow and wretchedness, she had wondered that Francisco had been taken: they had certainly swooped down unexpectedly; but still she had wondered.

But that was all forgotten now in this great rush of feeling. There was no room in the whole town for anything but joyful ebullience, an almost frantic merriment; and when Francisco burst through the shop in the evening a few days after his return, plunged into the back room where all the Fajals were sitting, and told them that he was going to marry Madeleine at once, they made little more than a general, formal objection.

There was a scene, of course. Nothing of that sort could possibly have passed without a scene of kinds: there was a fair amount of screaming, a very great deal of shouting all together, and some tears. But the elders did not really have their hearts in it, the strong-minded sister Mimi was away, and in the end tears were dried all round, and Francisco, late though it was, went off to see the mayor.

In the interval between this emotional evening and the marriage Dominique's objections were held in abeyance to a fair degree. She uttered some gloomy prophecies, but at the same time helped to prepare the clothes for the occasion with a lively pleasure. She defended the wedding against Mimi's protests with so many arguments that she nearly convinced herself, and she dismissed Mme. Roig's disapproval with a short and dry "If she does not like it, let her remain in her own house: that is all I say; let her remain in her own house."

She could not but admit that she had a handsome prospective son-in-law: he was well over six feet tall now, loose-limbed and gangling still with the contradictory grace of youth; his hair curled in black waves all over his head as it had done when he was a boy, but now there was an appearance of open, frank virility in his lean face. He had not come back from Germany so thin as some, not nearly, but he was lean, and he had a continual, appreciative appetite. It had been a little piping boy that Dominique had fed with caramels not so many years before, but now his big, deep barrel of a chest was filled with a thundering baritone, and when he sang the glasses hummed on the table. And yet, for all the virility in his face and for all the depth of his voice one would not have said that there was anything very manly there — the impression was certainly not that overwhelming masculine, beer-and-skittles, hairy impression that some men give. There was an admixture of sweetness, gentleness, or docility, something very un-like the desperate male carapace of tough-ness that the young men of Saint-Féliu put on with their breeches, a quality that could be described as wonderfully romantic or a trifle mawkish, according to the observer's sex or degree of liking for the man.

It was a hint, no more: nothing could be more inaccurate than to show him as a softy, or as anything like a softy, a young man who could be made game of with impunity by his fellows. He did not look like that at all. In any country he would have been reckoned a tall man, and here he towered over the little dark Catalans: and there was enough of his father — the old Camairerrou with a proved and shocking reputation — in his face to make it clear that you could not play with him.

As a son-in-law he had improved in his connections, by no effort of his own. Camairerrou had distinguished himself during the Occupation by drowning one of the occupying German soldiers and by taking to the mountains when the evacua-tion of Saint-Féliu was ordered: there, con-tinuing his trade of smuggling over the border, he had fallen in with an organization that passed refugees down into Spain, and knowing every path and cave in that wild neighborhood, knowing them even in the dark, he had been able to pass over several Allied airmen, secret agents, and Frenchmen bound for Algiers. Whenever it had been possible he had exacted a thumping great fee for his services, but when it had been clear that no money was to be had he had taken the men over for nothing. This, and the fact that when he had been paid he had invariably performed his bargain, redounded very much to his credit after the Liberation: so did the knowledge that somewhere in his house he had all the fees surrendered by his paying customers. He was still a lamentable father-in-law for Madeleine, but no longer an unmitigated disaster.

So they were married. They were married cheerfully, but with a background of gloomy muttering. They were married in the mairie with the tricolor, and in the temple with orange blossom, legally and sacramentally, and they were married in the Café de Gênes with dried sausage and anchovies, cakes and sweet wine, popularly.

Throughout the day, with the increasing effect of the wine and jollity, the forebodings of the elders had died down; but in the morning, with the wine quite gone and a general deflated sense of anticlimax abroad, they began again. They were ill-timed forebodings, intrusive and sometimes ill-natured; they were founded less on logic than on emotion, but they soon began to prove themselves to be true.

In the circumstances it would have been strange if they had not been true. The young couple lived in the upper part of a house belonging to the Fajals at the back of the town: it was a dank, narrow house stuffed into an interior angle of the fortifications, and the sun could not reach it at any time. The lower part of the house was a store, and the upper part had been arranged with the idea of letting it to summer visitors: but the scheme had been quite unsuccessful and for years the stiff, bright-yellow varnished wood furniture had stood rigidly on the shining linoleum, cold even in the flood of August. It was an unhappy arrangement: in the first generous flush the intention had been to give it unconditionally to Madeleine and Francisco as a home; but very soon the flush receded and as there had been no exact terms — nothing specified on either side — the elders began to withdraw the implied gift, until by the end of the year the place was little more than a set of furnished rooms where the young people were allowed to live.

It had begun simply enough: the women of the family had been naturally fascinated at running in and out of "Madeleine's apartment" as it was called at first, and naturally they came without invitation. They came to help her clean, sweep, and cook: her mother (an excellent cook) had taught her none of these things, but they were all very much surprised that she did not know how to do them by intuition. And they came, with the liveliest curiosity, to stare: there was little enough to see or know, but what little there was they wanted to see and know and talk about.

Then, when the disapproval of Francisco began to revive, they began to come into the house even more as by right; and her father, who surprised Madeleine by showing a greater jealousy of Francisco than the others, silently rearranged the furniture to his liking — replaced it in the positions it had occupied before the marriage.

It was a fairly slow process, this dispossession: it went on little by little, but it was nearly complete in twelve months. It was hardly a conscious process on either side; but on the side of the elders it was as efficient and unhesitating as if it had been carefully planned and concerted: more efficient.

However, the novelty, the romantic glow,

the conventional happiness carried Francisco and Madeleine through the first year. It was the second that brought so much conscious unhappiness. During the first year the sea, unfished for so long, yielded such quantities of fish that the oldest man had never seen the like, and the market, starved of fish for so long, was insatiable. There was plenty of money in Saint-Féliu, summer and winter, and even the *Amphitrite* earned enough to install an engine and to buy a lamparo, a little boat with a pair of huge lights to attract the fish by night, in the Spanish fashion.

But the next year was different. The summer was cold and unnatural and the anchovies stayed away from the coast altogether; even the sardines were very scarce, and somebody — the men of La Nouvelle, it was said — began dynamiting them. Soon everybody was doing it, scooping up the shattered little fish from the surface and hurrying furtively back to port: it could not last; not only did the preventive officers come, but the fish went clean away, and not all the motors or lamparos in Saint-Féliu would bring them back.

Madeleine and Francisco had, very early in their marriage, fallen into the habit of going to the family shop for meals. It had

begun with Madeleine's complete inca-
pacity — she really could not boil an egg at
first — and had continued because it was so
much easier and because Dominique loved
to have a talking crowd around the table. In
the first year it had been convenient; it had
not been necessary. Now it was essential,
and now Francisco and Madeleine arrived
with a hang-dog air, and now any quip or
jibe about their extravagance in the first
year's prosperity went home and rankled.
The quips and jibes, the "remarks passed"
were rarely meant to be as unkind as they
sounded sometimes, but it was remarkable
how accurately those rather stupid women
and that dull, heavy-witted man managed to
say just the thing that would hurt most
afterward, upon reflection.

They had been a little extravagant, it is
true: Madeleine had bought clothes; they
had often gone to Perpignan for the day,
and still more often to Collioure, where
Francisco's clever friends were to be found
on the beach or in the cafés; he had bought
canvases, colors, and a better easel. But it
had seemed at the time that no one thing
was more than a very little treat; there had
been no single example of unjustifiable ex-
pense, and after all, as they had said to one
another, a few hundred francs more or less

would not make a great difference by the end of the year.

It was not an agreeable situation, and it was less so for Francisco than it might have been for another, for his bad conscience made him vulnerable. He had not found casual work at the end of the fishing: he had not found it for the plain reason that he had not wanted to find it. He said to the family that it was not to be found (with a regretful shake of his head) and he had said to Madeleine that it was not to be found (with a grin of relief) and that he would have to pass the winter at home. They agreed that out of the evil came the blessing that he would have an uninterrupted stretch of time for his painting. He did: but it costs money to paint, and although the family could always be relied upon for help in kind, they would never part with cash.

Now Madeleine was glad that she had learned to type: she had never ceased seeing Mme. Roig in spite of the widow's disapproval of her marriage, and now she went and asked for her good offices with her nephew, Maître Roig, the lawyer, who sent most of his typing to a bureau in Perpignan. She, who had disliked the marriage too much to countenance it with a present, yet felt too much engaged by her use of Madeleine and by her interior promise, as well as by her affection for her, to feel at all easy, was very happy to do what Madeleine asked: she went at once, without stopping to put on her hat, and in ten minutes the thing was done. It proved an invaluable source of supply: it not only bought Francisco's materials and many of their meals, but it enabled him to spend a good part of his time with his friends at Collioure.

Painting is a messy business: it cannot be carried out in a shining little parlor where the position of each object is sacred. A room that is to be kept immaculate for wakes and marriages, the polished morgue of a self-respecting house, is not suitable; and there arose a great bitterness over the drops of paint, the smell in the room, and the wrongful displacement of the central table; for now Madeleine, typing at Me. Roig's, could not always be there to clean and to replace before one of her aunts or her mother got in.

Francisco took his easel to Collioure. His particular friends of the time had a very large attic where there was room for all to work, and there he took up his stand.

This was lonely for Madeleine, and when he took to sleeping there, it was more so. She did not tell her mother or anyone else —

she would never have done so at any time, but now that she was so withdrawn from them it would have been even less possible: for she was withdrawn from them, although Francisco blamed her for being entirely on their side, not with him at all: that was the root of all their quarreling.

She said as she lay there alone, watching the light of the street lamp swinging madly on the ceiling as the gale of the equinox took it, she said that it was better to watch it and know that he was on dry land than to watch it and think of him at sea. She said this, but she was saying it against her knowledge — a knowledge that she would not formulate or allow to appear whole, but which grew so substantial and familiar in those last weeks that she was not surprised, not fundamentally surprised, however cruelly shocked she was, when she came home one day from Me. Roig's house and found Francisco pale and strange in the middle of his possessions, packing them — his only. He spoke as if he were drunk, but he was not drunk. He had meant to get out alone, unseen; he had not thought he would be disturbed, and when he saw her he was uncertain what attitude to take. He had not prepared one. There was a terrible embarrassment between them, as if they were naked in front of strangers.

70

He saw that she did not intend to scream or fight and asked her to find his blue suit.

She said "Have you got your best shirts?"

He said "I took them last week," and after a second he flushed an ugly dark color, because he had lain with her since then.

She said "Do you want this?" It was her portrait that he had painted in the autumn. It was his best piece of work: it was framed. He said Yes, to put it by the other paintings stacked by the door; but he did not look and his voice was hardly recognizable.

They did not say anything more, and she went out of the room: she did not watch him pick up the load of things, the too-many parcels, bundles; go awkwardly out, down the stairs, put the things down, open the door, pick them up, and bolt out. His feet went sounding up the street, for he had shoes on; and in a minute the hollow wind slammed the door after him.

At the crossroads he jerked into the car, into the back seat, and the woman in front, after a glance at his face, started the engine and drove rapidly away on the white road of the coast.

He sat there in the back, abandoned to the movement of the car: he had never felt anything like this in his life. It was as if his whole being, the whole of the inside of his body, were bleeding, bleeding. The pain was something utterly beyond his experience.

It did not surprise him that his face was wet with tears: he leaned forward and let one roll on to the back of his hand.

What, what was he? A hero? Had he done something extremely brave? How terribly he was suffering: how terribly an artist must suffer. How shockingly wide is the range of an artist's feelings, he thought, only an artist could suffer so much: and the tears rolled on.

Chapter Three

"But, my dear Alain, how very yellow your face appears," she said, settling down comfortably, now that she had got him alone at last.

"My dear Aunt Margot," he replied, "I suppose it does."

"But, my dear Alain," she said in a kindly but serious tone, leaning forward and tapping him on the knee, "*why* is it so yellow?"

A vision of the Luong river, sliding dark and smooth in the suffocating gloom; the matted forest steaming in the thunderous rain; paddy fields, lichee trees, mushroom hats, flashed across his mind; but he despaired of his ability to describe the causes and the circumstances of his face's yellowness, and replied vaguely, "It is the climate, you know."

"The climate? Yes; and the food, no doubt. I cannot think that the climate has so much to do with it, or the people here would be blue, if not yellow and black as well. There never was such a disagreeable climate as this, with its unhealthy dryness and clouds of dust, and the dreadful wind that never stops except in midsummer, when you need it. This last winter . . . I am sure I was better off in the Pas-de-Calais, where at least it does not pretend to be warm, and where the houses are properly built for the winter. But Alain, you would be far better with a wife to look after your house and see that you are properly fed: these birds' nests and extraordinary dishes — mice, sharks' fins — I don't know indeed, but they cannot be good for you in the long run, however interesting at first, as curiosities."

"You are a friend to marriage, Aunt Margot: you rarely miss an opportunity of recommending me to take some young woman or other back with me. Yet the idea of Xavier having a wife again does not seem to please you?"

"Ah, that! No, indeed. And I am surprised that you should refer to it so lightly, Alain; if you knew how it grieved me, I am sure you would not do so."

"Tell me, has anything definite happened since you wrote to me last?"

"I wrote to you last in —" With her lips pursed and her eyes thrown up to the ceiling she numbered the days, weeks, months. "No. I cannot say that anything definite has happened, if you mean by that has he publicly announced that he is going to marry her, or has he been taken off in a strait jacket to the madhouse. That is where he would be if I had my way: I often tell him so. No: it has gone on in the same fashion, but now of course it is still more widely known. I have had letters of sympathy from Mme. Marty in Toulouse and from André at Constantine."

"I cannot see what it has to do with them. But when you say it is going on in the same fashion, what exactly do you mean? I have not gathered an exact impression: judging from Côme's remarks I should have supposed the girl to be a flaunting Jezebel, Xavier's acknowledged mistress — practically a common woman. But then, as I remember, she was very often with you before her marriage; and I cannot reconcile that with a very high degree of open depravity." He smiled tentatively, having intended to be a little facetious. However, his aunt frowned and said coldly, "No; I do not suppose you can." She paused; and then, with an air of almost masculine candor, quite characteristic of her, she said, "I do not know what Côme has said, but I should say that it is certainly untrue. This girl is not a bad girl at all. She sees her advantage, and she wishes to profit by it: that is all. If it were not that her gain is our loss, I should have nothing to say, nothing at all. But as it is . . . No. This question apart, I have nothing to say against Madeleine: indeed, I had a real affection for her. When she was a young girl I was very fond of her — too fond of her, perhaps — and when her good-for-nothing husband ran off I was exceedingly sorry for Madeleine. Even now I should be sorry if she were unhappy. No: I do not say that she is vicious or dishonest. But I do say that for us she is the enemy, and must be fought like one."

"So there is no moral issue?"

"Yes, there is a moral issue. She should not take advantage of Xavier's lunacy."

"Is she his mistress?"

"I do not think so. I cannot say, of course. From what I know of her I should say that she was virtuous; though it is true that she has a much more secretive nature than I liked, even then; and her marriage changed her a great deal. But I should certainly say that she is not his mistress, if for no other reason than that it would not answer her purpose. If it paid her to play the whore, it would be a different matter; though even then, I would not say for certain."

"You say that she takes advantage of Xavier's madness. I take it, then, that there is no inclination on her side — she does not care for him at all?"

"Care for him? Why of course not, Alain: how could you ask such a simple question? Think of Xavier's age and his appearance. He looks exactly like a dried old goat; you know he does. But of course, you never saw Francisco Cortade when he was grown up."

"The husband?"

"Yes. He was no good at all, no good whatever: but, my dear Alain, he looked like what's-his-name in the thing."

"Did he, though?"

"He did indeed. And still does, of course, wherever he is. He would make three of Xavier and still leave some to spare. A big, straight young fellow, very good-looking. Rather too good-looking for my taste, all gleaming teeth and curly hair, you know. But I must admit that he was not flashy, like most of the youths here who think themselves handsome, and he did not even look too much of a lout when he was dressed in his best clothes. He was not the sort who would wear well at all: no; there was too much youthful charm altogether; but he was exactly the kind of young man who would make a silly girl's heart turn right over. I could understand her perfectly well, although I never was a romantically inclined woman: and although I disapproved I thought that forty years ago I might have felt the same. I would never have acted as she did, of course; but I might have *thought* about it. And besides being so good-looking, he had that helplessness that is so appealing to an affectionate nature: that is to say, he *appeared* to have it. He *appeared* an ingenuous young man, too. However . . . No; I am convinced that Madeleine is eating her heart out for him. But even if she were not, I cannot see her looking at Xavier with anything but a businesslike eye. After all, he is twice her age, and even my dear sister-in-law, if she were alive now, could not call him anything but a dried-up old stick."

"Sometimes one finds girls madly enamored of men as old as their fathers. It is not so rare, either. And then again, Xavier is not actually decrepit, is he? If he were thinking of marrying, re-marrying, a handsome, well-connected dowry, are you sure that you would think of him as such an old man?"

"Well, perhaps not. But that really has nothing to do with the case, has it? There is no dowry or connection here."

"So she is entirely mercenary?"

"Yes. Though prudent would be a better

word. Prudential motives, they say, don't they? Though if we are to be entirely just to the girl I should say that I do not think she has her heart in the affair: I think it is mainly her family pushing her on. Though no doubt she sees her advantage as clearly as anybody."

"The family. That is the Pou-naous in the arcades."

"Yes. The father has the vineyard next to ours at the Puig d'en Calbo: there is not much harm in him. It is Mimi l'Empereur who is the dangerous one. She is Madeleine's aunt."

"I know her. Strong-minded woman."

"Yes. She always ruled that family — both the others have always been afraid of her — and she is the one who is pushing the girl on. Her motive is clear enough, of course."

"Has she some special motive?"

"You cannot have forgotten that old René l'Empereur is the one who has the tobacco license? Her father-in-law."

"No no. I know him well: a very agreeable old man. He was in the East for a long time and he loves to talk about it. I must go and see him soon. A very kind old man: he gave me a cigarette when I was twelve."

"No doubt. But he is mortal, nevertheless, and since the evacuation he has been

79

very infirm. Some day, probably quite soon, Mimi is going to want the license for herself or her husband. It is a thriving concern, and nowadays, since the war, there are so many people with claims to a tobacconist's license — resistants, deportees, victims of atrocities, and so on, as well as the wounded men and soldiers' widows — so many of them that Mimi will find it very difficult unless she has some real power to stand up for her. Xavier, of course, could arrange an affair of that kind in two minutes. She has courted him for years with her singing in the choir; but obviously this is a far better method of securing his interest."

"I thought the Pou-naous were Protestants."

"They are. But not Mimi: she was always a much more sensible woman than her sisters and she always preferred the church to the temple, even when she was a child. Then she quarreled with the old pasteur — something to do with the Christmas singing, I believe — and never went to the temple again. She was married in church."

"She never persuaded her sisters or Madeleine to leave the temple?"

"Oh no, there was no zealous, burning conversion, you know; she was just like the other people here — displeased with one, they drift to the other, but a *lukewarm* drift. No, her sisters, especially Thérèse (Dominique never goes anywhere) continued to go to the temple: sometimes Madeleine would be in the church — she helped Mimi decorate the chapels sometimes — but in general she went to the temple, and she was married there."

"That's bad."

"From the point of view of Xavier, you mean? Yes. There would have been little danger if she had been married properly: I will say this for Xavier, he is not one of your modern, lax, easy-going Catholics. And even now I do not think he would put his principles aside, mad though he is."

"No doubt you are right. But tell me, how did it all begin? That is what I have never understood from your letters."

"It began very simply. When her husband left her she was very, very unhappy. Her family would not leave her alone for a second, and she often came to see me, not so much for comfort as for refuge. I was foolish enough to encourage her to spend more and more time typing for Xavier — occupation and distraction, I thought. I say I was foolish enough to do so, and if you wish to be very modern and clever you may say that is why I resent the present situation so bitterly. I would not own this to anyone else, Alain, but I was a fool, a fool." She clasped her hands with exasperation. "I never thought for a moment — but of course I *should* have thought. Xavier was handling her divorce, and I suppose the scabrous details excited him. I can think of no other explanation: he has always been a cold, bloodless sort of a man, the model of rectitude. You could have left him alone with — with — oh, with any form of temptation that even Côme could imagine, with his obscene library that he thinks nobody knows about."

"Her divorce? How does that agree with her eating her heart out for him?"

"It was her father. He was like a wild boar with anger: he was at Xavier's house the moment he heard of it — that was a week or ten days after Francisco had gone. She had kept it to herself all that time, and it was only because Francisco had left a paper at the mairie and the mairie people talked that the family heard about it at all."

"What in the world did he want to leave a paper at the mairie for?"

"Oh, to state that he was deserting Madeleine and that he was entirely at fault, so that there could be a divorce without any difficulty. It is the usual thing."

"Oh? I did not know."

"Well, as soon as he had this paper he was round at Xavier's door, roaring like a lion. It is entirely his doing, the divorce. He is paying for it, of course, and he keeps pressing Xavier to hurry it on, whatever it costs. They are afraid that she would have him back if he were to return."

"That would be a solution."

"He would never dare come back. Her father would kill him. His own father, old Camairerrou, said he would hold him for Jean Pou-naou to stab where he liked."

"Could she not go to him?"

"If she knew where he was she could; at least, in theory. But I have no doubt that she would much rather be burnt alive than do so."

"Oh." (A pause.) "You were telling me how it began."

"Yes. That was the situation, you understand: the girl wretchedly unhappy, running away from anyone who wanted to talk about the affair (and it was the best piece of gossip they had had in the town for a very long time) shut up for hours with Xavier, who is, at least, a quiet and tactful man. And there is Xavier, suddenly brought into contact with a girl in a wild, devil-may-care state of mind, abandoned and (perhaps I wrong him) easily to be taken advantage of. He has her for hours at his side, while he is dealing with these papers that must, I presume, raise carnal ideas in his mind. And at the same time I am sitting here like a fool, having encouraged the disaster to take place.

"And then, when the mischief was done, I began to hear things. Tongues must have been wagging before, for by the time that I heard the beginning of the scandal it was quite well-formed, not mere dribs and drabs of guesswork. You do not have to tell me that it was ill-natured, malicious gossip by ignorant, idle, foolish women: I know that perfectly well. And I know, too, that when gossip has a certain ring it is always true: if you were an old woman, Alain, and if you had gossiped as much as I have, you would know that ring, and you would not think that you could dismiss an unpleasant piece of news just by saying, 'Oh, it's only gossip.' " Alain made a disclaiming gesture, and his aunt went on, "Xavier moved his rooms around: he changed his study to the room in the corner of the courtyard on the left of the door, you know? and moved his clerk into a room on the other side of the hall, and he had the typewriter put into the little room behind his new study. It made me very uneasy, this new arrangement, and I hinted to Xavier that it might be unfortunate for Madeleine if there were any gossip about her. He made no reply and I noticed that he was much more carefully dressed than usual. I think I must have chosen my moment very badly. About a week later I asked him, apropos of a novel about a legal family, whether it was not very dangerous for a lawyer to have an affair with a woman who was also his client. He said Yes, it was; very. He knew perfectly well what I meant, and he was so angry in his silent way that I was on edge with alarm. However, I gathered all my forces and asked him whether he knew what was being said. He did not answer. But on the Thursday that followed, in the evening, he said that it would be a foolhardy imbecile who would meddle with *his* affairs, and that he would have the greatest pleasure in the world in laying a man by the leg, or a woman or a child, laying them by the leg for the rest of the term of their natural lives, if they dared tattle about him.

"I learned in the morning that Marinette — really, she has very little sense, although she is your aunt — had been so criminally stupid as to go to the shop and have a long talk with Dominique and Thérèse Pounaou. She had not consulted me, of course: and of course all she accomplished was to put ideas into their heads and to set them on. They may not be very intelligent (though they are certainly cleverer than your Aunt Marinette) but they know enough to come in out of the rain, or to try to pick up a piece of gold if they see it lying in the gutter. And of course, her stupid, interfering visit came back to Xavier's ears almost as soon as she had left.

"It was some time after that, quite a long time, that Xavier asked me whether I remembered asking him about the relations of a lawyer and his female client. I said that I did, and I knew that he was going to say something horribly unpleasant; but then he said 'There is nothing in the code of the profession, nothing whatsoever, that prevents a lawyer from marrying his client.' At that horrible word marriage, Alain, I really thought I was going to faint. I have never done so except once, at the Roubaix station when I was a girl, but I remembered the feeling again immediately. But, however, I sat down, and it passed off."

Alain was about to make some remark, or at least a sympathetic noise, when she went on. "In another man it might just have been a rash fling, almost meaningless — but you know Xavier. He had been vexed, no doubt, by the family meeting that day. We were all gathered here, and he must have seen the

86

others arriving: even if he did not see them, he must have heard them. The house sounded as if it had been filled with parrots. Thomas began screeching in Catalan, as he always does when he is excited, and I went out into the garden, and, my dear, the noise was terrible, even there. It frightened the cats."

Aunt Margot had lived for fifty years among the Catalans, but like a true French-woman she spoke no word of their language, remained impenetrably sealed against its daily influence; and she had raised the standard of spoken French in the family to a high pitch of correctness. Only her brother-in-law Thomas — the backward Thomas Menjé-Pé — still lapsed into barbarisms in her presence, and even, under great stress, into his native idiom.

"Upon my word," said Alain, shifting uneasily in his chair, "I must say that I sympathize with Xavier for being angry. As far as I can gather from the others, they all seem to have had a go at him at one time or another, and every single one of them has had the same brilliant idea of attacking the girl, assuring him that she is practically a whore and that he is a fool. No: I would not be at all surprised if he did not marry her out of hand, merely to vex his relations. And after all, would it be such an unmixed disaster, this marriage?"

"Oh, Alain! You have quite a good brain, and yet you can ask me a question like that. Would you be pleased? Were you pleased when first you heard of it?"

"Well, no; I was not. In fact, I thought it was a grave misfortune. I still think it would be most undesirable, but I do not quite see it in the same awful light as you do. Tell me, Aunt Margot, just what is so disastrous about it? This is supposed to be a democratic country — and it is the most truly democratic that I have ever seen, even counting England and America — but even if it were not, we Roiges are not so very different from the Fajals. After all, my great-grandfather worked his vineyards just like any other peasant, and probably he fished in the same boat as Madeleine Pou-naou's great-grandfather. I dare say they were cousins."

"Oh dear, Alain: I am really too old to be attacked now with fine romantic theories. What you say is very noble and quite true; but it has no bearing on the matter in hand, has it, my dear? So you will forgive me if I do not tell you how I know that two and two make four. There is just one aspect of the disaster that I will touch upon: you know something about Xavier's political interests in the region, do you not?"

"Yes."

"I do not suppose you know much, my poor Alain, cooped up in that nasty laboratory with germs — very like a monk. I wish you had had a vocation; it would have suited you admirably well, and it might have been very valuable to have another cleric in the family. However, I dare say you had some knowledge of the state of affairs under the Third Republic."

"Yes. Politics stank."

"They were unclean. You should not have said 'stank' to me, Alain."

"I beg your pardon: unclean."

"But we are not concerned with judging them. Clean or unclean, they were *intricate:* and now they are just the same, only more intricate. Influence depends on a thousand combinations, ten thousand little points — the innumerable right contacts and relations, the always having been influential, the being respected by a great many people. Until this began, Xavier had all that. He was respected by a great many people, and the reason why he was respected was not only because of his money, or the family's money, nor because of his clean hands — though that was important — but chiefly for his astuteness. He was known far beyond the region as an astute lawyer, excellent at a settlement out of court; an astute man of business, placing the family's money to great advantage; and as an astute politician, able to manage and combine conflicting interests and to conduct the election campaigns to the admiration of all. It is their respect for his astuteness that enables him to get what he wants from Paris without paying too much for it — which increases their respect, of course. But what happens to his astuteness if he is taken in by a chit of a village girl and a family of impecunious grocers? Drawn into a marriage that would make even the simplest mountain peasant laugh? An immoral liaison with the girl would shock and displease many of his clients and some of his right-wing political associates; it would certainly damage him, but it would not greatly affect the majority of the electors: marriage with her would be totally different. Such a marriage! No: ridicule still kills in this country, and his reputation for astuteness and all his prestige would vanish directly in a great howl of derision. Politically he would sink like a stone. Already I don't know how much harm has been done: six months ago he could appoint our deputy; now I am by no means sure that he could be certain of having a man elected to the departmental council. In six months' time, if this goes on, they will be laughing in his face at a municipal meeting and making the sign of horns behind his back. Then where will we be? Where will Gaudérique's appointment in Africa be? Will your people feel so sure of their laboratory's subsidy?

"But if I were to try to explain all these things to you there would never be an end." She was growing hoarse, but she could not resist adding, "Just think of one single instance — Xavier's interest with the right-wing, old-fashioned Church party: I have been a great help to him there, and I still am; but I could not uphold him for a moment, even the bishop could not, if he were to marry a divorced Protestant. Think of it: think of the Church influence lost. You know what it is, even in these miserable days, and even in an atheistic province like this. But there really will be no end if I go on, and my throat is hurting already from talking so much."

"You must try to come down to our base world, Alain," she said a little later, pouring him out a glass of wine. "We must deal with things as they are."

Alain drank half his wine, and remained staring gravely at what was left. "Yes," he said, nodding at the glass, "of course it is quite impossible. I only thought . . . This is very good rancio: is it ours?"

"It is Xavier's, from the Puig d'en Calbo. You know, Alain, if Xavier were to marry that girl, and she were to make him leave her the vineyard at the Puig d'en Calbo (which she certainly would try to do, to reunite it with the Fajals' land) I think I should burst in my grave. Hercule had such difficulty in getting it from old Pou-naou, and the whole family thought it such a triumph when he succeeded. It took him twenty years."

"Yet what can one do about it? Xavier is not a minor, nor a lunatic."

"Oh but he is, Alain. Far madder — Alain, could you not certify him? Do: it would give us all such pleasure."

"It would hardly improve his reputation."

"At least it would safeguard his property."

"But, seriously, what can one do?"

"You should use your influence with Xavier. You should go to him and say —"

"No. I mean seriously. You said just now that we must deal with things as they are: very well: we both know how much my eloquence is likely to do. Have you any clear idea of a way of stopping Xavier from making a fool of himself?"

"No," she said, a little ruffled, "if you put it like that, I cannot say that I have. But you underestimate your influence with Xavier, I assure you."

"Is it so great that he would stop doing what he very much wants to do just for my sake?"

"Perhaps not. No: I do not suppose that it is, really. But I had been relying on you to do something, Alain."

"I am sorry for that. You will be disappointed, and then you will think me a tiresome fellow, you know." He walked to the window and looked across the road to Xavier's house; for a few moments of silence he looked at the house with a steady, critical gaze, trying to assess it as a stranger might — a stranger with a difficult interview awaiting him inside. It was a substantial house, three sides of a square, with iron railings, tall ones, finishing the square on the pavement side; a flagged court with oleanders and bushy lemon trees in tubs, a stone bench with a table in the shade of the lemons. The court was rather crowded with all this vegetation and in the winter it would no doubt look somewhat dank and somber; but now in the sunlight it looked well enough; indeed, to a passer-by on the dusty, reverberating road it stood as an inviting oasis of shade and coolness. The tall windows, one on each side of the front door, a row of three above; they, and the flanking windows in the wing that met the sun, were all shuttered against the flood of light; long, gray shutters that gave the house a reserved and noncommittal air. Only the inside angle on the left escaped the sun, and there the windows were open.

For a moment it seemed to him that he was about to seize the meaning of the house's look in spite of its reserve, but then, almost while the thought was forming into a pattern of words, the impression dissolved and was lost in the soft, easy lines of familiarity. He knew the place too well to see it whole, and now he had lost the power that his absence had given him. For an instant it vexed him so much that he was on the point of unhanging the big looking-glass on the wall, walking with it to the window and standing there with his back to the street to look at the house, but the house reflected, to recapture in the unfamiliar change of balance that sense of comprehension that he had lost, to recapture it as one may recapture the freshness of a picture in a mirror or the outside world's view of your lover's face, seen daily to obliteration. But it would have startled his aunt; and what exactly did he hope to gain? She would ask him that, and he would find it impossible to answer.

From one of the open windows in the shade there came a steady high tapping. "She is there now," said the old lady, standing at Alain's side and looking over the road with him.

"Oh, she still goes there?"

"Yes; she goes there still. Did you suppose that she did not?"

"It was stupid of me, but I think I did. I had thought of it as a closed chapter, a part of history; and the present state of affairs appeared to be proceeding on different lines. I am not sure what I supposed exactly, but I do not think that a typewriter entered into it. That was what I was asking you at the beginning, now I come to think of it, but we strayed off on to all manner of subjects."

"Yes, she goes there every day. That has not changed at all, and she still types just as hard as ever, which is very strange. Do you not find it very strange, Alain?"

"It sounds as though Xavier were either not very ardent or else a curiously business-like lover. I should like to see her."

"You will have to wait until the evening, then, when she goes: you will see nothing from here. Nothing," she added, with a note of vexation that made her nephew smile.

"Is she handsome?"

"You will have to judge that for yourself. Some people affect not to think so. I used to think that she was quite the prettiest girl I had ever seen in my life; but I think you have to feel kindly toward people to find them beautiful — at all events, since this has started I have thought her looks have gone down and down. But you will see her soon, no doubt. You go to Xavier's on Tuesday, do you not?"

"Yes, on Tuesday. I am not sure that I altogether look forward to it. But now," he said, looking at the clock among the bronze mermaids, "I have to go and see Aunt Marinette and Uncle Joseph."

"My poor Alain, you have a dull evening ahead of you. Marinette will tell you all that I have just told you, whether you like it or not; and she will take much longer over it, with her profound reflections. However, you will conduct yourself very well, I am sure, and it will not last much longer than three hours, because they always go to bed at ten now. You will give them my love, won't you?"

"I will not forget."

The heat outside struck him like a soft wave; the heat of the air was all round him, and as he moved out of the shade the direct sun clapped him on the back. It warmed his thin body through to the bones, and with a sensuous pleasure in the heat he walked down the middle of the road, where the sun struck hottest. After so many tropical years his blood, or the mixture of lime juice and quinine that passed for blood, was as thin as a lizard's, and here at Saint-Féliu even in the summer a little coldness lingered in his body, to be dispelled only by the straight blast of the sun itself. The sun agreed with him: he liked it — not, perhaps, the immoderate degree of sun that weighed on Prabang before the rains, but sun within reason. It certainly agreed with him, for whereas many of his colleagues had run mad, or had returned home early as confirmed invalids, he had lasted years and years with no more than malaria: others again had been equally lucky in escaping disease, but many of them were swollen with drink, horribly obese through no fault of their own, for the drinking was obligatory; but Alain had that kind of body that goes thin and yellow in the heat, and now, with his frail, attenuated hands, and his lean, hollow-cheeked face he had an ascetic, other-worldly air — a very well-bred monk by Zurbarán. This air belied him; for although he was by nature and inclination somewhat reserved, or withdrawn, he was by no means an ascetic; in his quiet and reflective manner he had a strong tendency toward jollity; and as he was the first to admit, in his republican way, he was not at all well bred. And he was not well bred, by arms or by the Almanach de Gotha, for all his people on both sides were peasant stock; but he looked very well, a small, straight, well-compounded figure, with a round, brown head and the short, beak-like nose of the mountain Catalans. It was a face that would wrinkle with distinction in his age.

He went down to the Place; it was almost the first time since he had arrived that he had been alone, and even at the cost of being late at his Aunt Marinette's house, he intended to make a private homecoming pilgrimage. From the Place he walked up the narrow arcades, a street where the houses stood almost touching overhead, and where the shops filled the arched-over pavement with baskets of brilliant fruit and vegetables. Opposite the Fajals' shop he hesitated, looked in under the arch, beyond the foreshop into the shop behind, where in the fly-blown gloom a little crowd of old black women stood croaking among the stockfish. He had a minute's mind to go in, but he dismissed the thought and went on up the street, under the Virgin's balcony, where a staring little doll with carmine cheeks stood in the middle of a quantity of lace and glass jewelry holding a plaster baby: she still had the same villainous tin crown, but the balcony had been repainted and now, behind the tinsel and glass, one could see something of the delicate stone tracery in which the original statue had been placed, five hundred years before — a statue that had been indignantly rejected as old-fashioned in 1865. That made him think of Aunt Margot: if she had been the leading woman of the church at that time she would have done just the same: with the approval of one and all she would have had the old stone out and replaced it with a plaster image from Saint-Sulpice. There was an odd contradiction. She was one of those women who seem born for the role of a sharp old lady; a strongly independent character; a little crotchety, but never foolish; far from womanly, yet equally far from being masculine; a being apart, self-contained, a product of no obvious sequence of development: you could not imagine her a child, nor a young woman, and only by stretching the term to its uttermost could you see her as even middle-aged. In most people you can detect the remnant of an earlier age or foresee the shape of an age that is to come: they are not wholly submerged in the age of their years, their actual childhood, youth, or age. In a little boy lost in a book one can see the form of the man; and looking sideways at the unconscious, released, upturned faces of one's neighbors at the cinema one may see the surviving adolescent repeated and repeated, open-mouthed, in diminishing perspective to the end of the row. But there was nothing of this in Aunt Margot: she was an old lady, and probably she had been one since she was forty-five. She was a widow, and she wore a widow's weeds from long habit, but she had nothing of the look of a once-married woman: she had recovered her maidenhood and dried it. There was no nonsense about her: she was devout, and she had a genuine sense of piety and religion; but she would discuss Church politics with a freedom that would have surprised an anti-clerical. There was no nonsense about her: yet in matters of church decoration, plaster saints, and devotional books, her judgment was obscured, her taste fled or became womanish in the worst sense, and her reason refused its aid.

It was a contradiction that Alain found insoluble: he had found it so from his earliest days, when at the first dawn of aesthetic perception he had seen her supervising the emplacement of a brand-new Saint Expédit in the parish church.

He passed by his cousin's salting house and hurried through the reek of anchovies: from the huge brown cave filled with barrels came the girls and women, hurrying away at the end of their day's work. The older women recognized him and called "Good evening, Monsieur Alain," and "Are you going for a walk, Monsieur Alain?" He hurried; he could still decently avoid them. He called back "Good evening. Yes, a walk. Good evening, Marie, Josette . . ." Another time, the next time, he would stop and talk, but this evening he would permit himself to hurry on.

They were good women; excellent, kind women: but why were they so ugly? Their dress had a great deal to do with it, black, light-drinking black; black stockings and black espadrilles: with the girls it was the same, tallow-white faces, short thick bodies wrapped in frocks of undetermined color, then a short stretch of corpse-white calf, and dull blue cloth shoes. Never any freshness, even in their first youth: what was the matter? Why were they so ugly when the men were so fine, straight and brown, brilliantly colored in the sun? How was it that he had not seen a single pretty girl in his walk so far? And what a pity it was, they being such an embellishment to the day.

Perhaps Aunt Margot had caught something of this sorrowful influence, this natural inclination toward ugliness?

But looking up he saw a young woman coming down the slope toward him, and he said "My God."

"My God," he said, internally. "Here's freshness; here's bloom. Here's the lovely sin of the world."

In his own village a man of a certain standing cannot leer at young women in the street, and the smile that unexpected pleasure had brought to Alain's face was not a leer. It lacked the element of carnal invitation. It was nothing but the expression of his appreciation; but a superficial observer might have misinterpreted it.

She was coming down the steep, cobbled hill, and the leaning back, the poising of her high heels on the uneven stones and her higher position accentuated the straightness of her carriage; it made her look tall: she was little over the middle height, but there she looked far taller. She was aware that he was looking at her; the fixed unconsciousness of her face showed that, and he was aware that he was prolonging his stare to rudeness and beyond. He blew his nose to cover a slight degree of confusion and walked on up the hill, faster, and when they had passed with averted gaze he did not look back.

Was that a local girl? There were a few summer people staying in rooms, but she had more the look of a Spaniard or a Catalan. She was not dressed like a holiday person: what was she dressed in? He could not recall. Something ordinary, no doubt, or at all events not so remarkable that one would notice it with that face to look at. Charming, charming, he thought, still smiling at the recollection, a recollection of clear line, freshness, cleanliness, blossom: delightful.

He was climbing the steep lane behind the school now, and still thinking about the elegant young woman. Was she perhaps the cause of all the tumult? An efficient cause, indeed, if she were. And with this thought he came to the wall. Here was the part of Saint-Féliu farthest from the sea, and here the wall and the tower were unencumbered by houses: he walked up the hollow-worn steps to the rampart and along to the tower. He reached the low arch, and bent and cautious in the dark he felt his way up the spiral staircase; he passed the well-remembered broken step, and now he was in the brilliant sunshine, on the round platform, high above the town and sea and country.

There were seven towers, one at each angle of the wall, but this was the tallest and the best: it was also the only tower into which one could go without the disgust of filth and rubbish, for not only was it withdrawn from the houses, but the path at its foot led nowhere — had no traffic at all. It was an ancient tower, and the breastwork on which he leaned was crumbling fast, but it was modern compared with the wall. Parts of *that* were of immense antiquity — huge boulders dragged and piled by some unimaginable, brutish effort — then there was the later work, crudely dressed early medieval masonry, enormously solid: but these very old parts of the wall were not to be seen for its whole length; sometimes they wandered off and were to be found in the middle of the town, serving as the walls of houses, or even standing incongruously alone; for at different times Saint-Féliu had grown, and with its uneven, unsymmetrical growth the wall had worked outward. Now it stood in a curve that made rather less than half a circle, each end resting on the sea shore: "curved," one says, for that was the general effect, but exactly speaking it was a series of lines, with a tower at each angle. It was a satisfactory wall in that it enclosed the town, and it was eminently beautiful; but it was not a useful wall. The town was commanded on three sides by the heights inland, and perhaps it was for this reason that the wall had shown no development later than the use of cannon-balls. Even Vauban, that indefatigable improver, had left it alone, and the wall, with its crenellated towers, continued to crumble and to mellow through his century to this, growing less efficient and more beautiful each year.

Leaning there on the parapet, hooked on to it by his elbows so that his shoulders were hunched up to his ears, Alain looked not unlike a gargoyle staring out over the town. He passed it carefully over in review, looking for changes and for known, personal landmarks. It was exactly as he remembered it, as he thought of it when he was far away, exactly the same and yet with an additional strength of life, a vibrant immediacy: his memory, however sentimental with the distance, might not have provided the shrilling of the cicadas in the oleaster that grew tortuously from a crevice in the wall below, the play of the dancing, shimmering air, the flick and dart of the lizards, and the distant sound of men hauling on a boat. The hun-

dred roofs below him tilted in every conceivable plane, a pink mass, shaded,
lichened, faded to innumerable variations,
following no apparent order or plan. From
this angle he could see no streets, and it was
only by known trees, balconies, an occa-
sional roof garden, that he could guide the
flight of his spirit over Saint-Féliu. There,
where the big cloud of old green lay at the
bottom of the town, was the Place — the
huge plane trees tired and dusty in the heat.
To the left and up the hill there was the
darker green of the oranges in his cousin
Côme's garden: a little nearer again there
were the brilliant blue shutters and the palm
trees that stood behind the arcades. The arcades, where that girl lived. No, she lived by
herself under the wall. His eye ran round the
curve, past the next tower, past the gap
where the Germans had destroyed the arch
of the Banyuls gate, past that and to the returning angle, where he fixed the roof, fixed
it to within two or three houses, and stared
hard at it, as if he might draw some knowledge from its tiles.

Then flying back across the town to the
white shape of Xavier's house, he brooded
there, gazing on the roof that covered his
cousin: it was the only slated roof in the
whole swarm of them; slated, cold, urban

106

and aloof. After some minutes his glance wavered, turned momentarily to his Aunt Margot's — a high-thrown magnolia and green shutters against the white walls, wrought-iron balconies — and then sped away to the right-hand extremity of the town, pausing in its flight along the shore at a figure on the jetty. A figure with a white hat. Yes, that would be his Uncle Thomas, called Menjé-Pé, a fanatical fisherman: he was fishing now. He was one of the few in the family who still had a current nick-name, Fish-eater, and who did not mind it: for most of the family the called-names had been left behind a generation ago. But Menjé-Pé was something of a throwback; was it because he always spoke Catalan or was it because he was a little simple that they still called him Menjé-Pé? Not the latter, for Uncle Joseph was gaga, and he had no nickname. He was flailing about. Had he caught something? No. In all proba-bility he had just caught up his hook and lead and lost them. Sixty years ago Menjé-Pé had started fishing; he was fourteen then, and he had the zeal and the lack of skill of his age. He still had the same zeal, but somehow he had avoided gaining any skill: he caught nothing but idiot fish.

On along the shore, past the wall where it

reached the sea, past the dry river-bed to the faubourg, the extension of Saint-Féliu that lay beyond the walls. It was not the new town, as it would have been in most places: it had always been there, but in the old days, when the walls were so frequently manned against the Algerines and Tangerines and Salee rovers, the faubourg had no buildings of value — net lofts, places for storing wood, little barbarous naked houses, no more — and still it remained the poorest quarter, where the fishermen lived pell-mell in a romantic slum. His gaze hunted about the faubourg: somewhere there lived old Camairerrou, the absconding husband's father. A wicked old man he was too, by all accounts. It was Camairerrou who had stabbed the Spanish frontier guard: and more.

The dark legend of the infamous En Jepetou, great-uncle to Camairerrou, was in his mind; but the constriction of his chest against the stone called him back to the present. He stood up, brushed the dust of stone from his coat, and turned round. For the hundredth time the theatrical contrast surprised an expression of wonder from him: here, dense town, thousands of incessantly moving lives huddled close together; there, the silent hills. For the first moment it was a complete and absolute contrast, but then it began to be diluted by the laborious vineyards, market-gardens by the river-bed, squares of cork oak, and the peppering of tiny stone huts like boxes all over the nearer hills; diluted still more by the railway line that plunged out of a black-rimmed hole, and by the half-dozen angular villas of the richer salters and wine merchants, perched up beyond the railway. Still, the farther hills remained as untouched as the sea; high, remote, arid, dark and sterile, poisoned with the sun.

The villas were a pity: they were all recent, pretentious and obtrusive. The most pretentious, the thing with an abortive tower like an excrescence and magenta shutters, was Aunt Marinette's. His apéritif would be waiting for him there already; and somewhere under that ugly roof Angélique would now be cooking a dinner, a dinner — ah. Mentally he kissed his gathered fingers and threw the kiss into the air, and with the thought of dinner brilliantly vivid in his mind he turned and hurried down the tower.

Chapter Four

Xavier. He was a tall man, taller than his cousin, a tall, thin, gray man. It was not his hair but his face that was gray, and his eyes; pale, almost colorless eyes under black hair, that gave his expression a disquieting frigidity even when he was at his most cordial.

It was that more than anything else perhaps that had made Alain feel uneasy in his company and inferior to him when he was younger — that cold, dispassionate eye. It seemed to remove them one from the other by more than the wall of years. But there were very many other circumstances: for one, nothing he had ever been able to do had ever impressed Xavier, and if he tried to reproduce some of the clever things they said at the hospital where he studied, the brilliance always dissipated and the remarks came out with a bald naivety that was painful to the young Alain. He had been second fiddle in those days. There had been no struggle, no vying. Xavier had his superiority quite secure, for he did not care about it in the least. He had been a superior young man altogether; but Alain had never disliked him for that. Xavier had never showed the hateful marks of a prig, and Alain, then a candid, affectionate youth, had admired his lean good looks, his clear, incisive brain, and his self-contained undeferential efficiency, his detachment. If it had not been for one thing, however, perhaps it would have been impossible for Alain to have liked this paragon — the passer of examinations, the model of correctness, good behavior, and application. The saving grace was that Alain knew very well, as the whole family knew, that Xavier's father was an evil-tempered man, powerful, domineering, and restless; a ferocious domestic bully. It was not that Alain blamed his Uncle Hercule then; he accepted him as a force of nature and hated him without forming any judgment; but he was sorry for Xavier, and would have said so if ever they had been intimate enough. There was something very moving, in those days, in the sight of that proud, cold young man being humiliated and bully-ragged, and bearing it with a pale, masked fortitude.

Now Xavier was rid of his father; now there was no reason to be sorry for him; and now his superiority should have been without alloy, for he had developed in the way that his friends had hoped, and now he was not only the chief man of Saint-Féliu but one of the outstanding men of the province — too good for the provinces, but willing to remain there and rule rather than become a subordinate in Paris. But his superiority no longer oppressed Alain: Dr. Roig was not an outstanding figure in tropical medicine — not nearly as distinguished in his field as Xavier was in the law and politics — but he knew the value of his work, and he could look upon the family's phoenix without feeling any undue reverence. The knowledge that the phoenix was an errant fowl helped a little, too.

At this moment the phoenix (a suspicion that he might be able to make an epigram about cuckoos, phoenixes, and fornication drifted across the surface of Alain's mind) was bent over a heap of papers among the ruins of their dessert: he was running down a column of figures, double-checking them. These were the figures to do with his stewardship of Alain's patrimony: three vineyards in part-ownership, two houses in the town and half a house in the faubourg, the bigger share of a cork oak wood, two olive groves, one mill. It was not the income that Xavier was calculating — Alain had had that with exact punctuality, and it was all gone in equipment, a new microscope, more equipment, and the indulgence of a trip to Macao to buy a Chinese painting — not the income, but the yield, to see whether Alain's theory of mulching did in fact increase the number of grapes on a vine economically and without lowering the strength of the wine. It was a long task, and Xavier's attention was wholly absorbed: Alain could stare at him without disguise. He was easier to see with a stranger's eye than his house had been. The years had done more to him, so very much more. It was a big-featured face; all the room was taken up by his nose, mouth, and the deep sinking of his eyes; the features seemed to have coarsened very much. It was the kind of face that gave the impression, as Aunt Margot said, of having been slowly dried, dried without heat. Thick skin — liverish? A strong blue beard shading all the lower half. It was not an attractive face.

Xavier had always had a hard, closed, self-contained expression, and now his face was deeply marked with it: hardness, acuity, and the habit of concentration were stamped there. As he sat opposite to Alain with the papers in front of him he looked the very image of undeviating purpose; even there at his own table, after a long and excellent

113

dinner, he sat with a certain rigidity of his shoulders that showed a mind square, angular, exact and unrelaxing. He was dark and high in his chair, dark in his black coat; the only color in him was the tiny crimson fleck of the Légion d'Honneur in his buttonhole: an imposing figure, looked at from most angles; and from others perhaps a faintly comic one. Though it would have been a brave man who continued to find Xavier comic with Xavier looking at him: from any angle at all he was a formidable creature. One did not take liberties with Xavier.

Yet this was the man who was proposing to indulge a middle-aged folly at a price that would . . . It was difficult to believe it at all, sitting there face to face with bourgeois integrity personified, the incarnation of unremitting attention to the family interest. It was not the folly that was surprising: any man at the sight of youth gone, gone forever, is liable to break out in a last desperate fling, looking for his lost years in a young thing's bed. Though it was surprising, too: surprising in Xavier. His rigidity, his strength of discipline, appearance, everything, should by rule have been betrayed (if this time had to bring him idiocy) into some secret darkness at Perpignan: but even that, so commonplace, so ordinary and unremarked in

114

dirty Côme for example, would have been unexpected in Xavier. Apart from anything else, Alain, looking at that gray, concentrated face, the hard, calculating eyes behind the black-rimmed spectacles, could not see the rigid lines ever dissolving into the shapes required by the tender passion — or indeed any passion but anger. And then again, against the likelihood of strange whorings in Perpignan, there was the fact of Xavier's piety. To those who knew him well, it was the cardinal fact in his character: at one time Alain, pluming himself on the cynical penetration that now seemed so callow, had attributed it to policy, policy with regard to Aunt Margot's private fortune, and above all policy with regard to the Church interest. For although Xavier inherited from his father his membership — influential membership — of the anti-clerical Radical-Socialist party, he was nevertheless able to dispose of most of the votes of the churchgoers. He owed this uncommon power in part to family connection and to the local impotence of the right-wing or clerical parties, but far more to his acknowledged excellence as a churchman: so it was not unnatural for Alain, younger then, to tap his nose with a knowing smirk. But now the callowness was outgrown — had been these many years — and now Alain, standing by his cousin in church, could respect and admire, though he could not imitate, the cold, rapt fervor on Xavier's face. It had almost frightened him, the first time he saw and understood that sudden glimpse of Xavier naked.

Xavier wrote in pencil on the margin, added; drummed his fingers and shuffled back through the pages.

Now Alain was thinking along another line, wondering what there could be that was sympathetic in the man on the other side of the table: was it anything more than custom that sat them down opposite to one another, and kept them talking of their common affairs? Custom and mutual interest? Was there any degree of voluntary friendship, free association? It would be interesting to ask Xavier what he thought: he would not return a sentimental answer, at all events.

Xavier looked up suddenly; there was a rare, benevolent look on his face, and as he took off his glasses his eyes lacked their usual stony glint. The suddenness of his regard and its unexpected cordiality threw feelings of surprise and guilt into Alain's mind: he returned the smile with a certain effort.

"I should say offhand," said Xavier, "that

it has made no difference at all. I cannot commit myself to a definite opinion, of course, but that is my general impression. There were a few more Chasselas, but there were rather less on the Grenaches. The trouble is that there are so many imponderables: old Joanole did not have his heart in the experiment, for one thing. He said, from the first, that it was madness to try to change the ways of our fathers. It might have been different if he had brought more good will to the task."

"Oh, it was in no way a scientific experiment. For that we should have established controls, and it would have to go on over a period of years. No, it was only an idea. But I shall remain convinced that the earth itself is improved. Have you the figures there for the new plantation?"

"Yes, I have," he replied with some hesitation. "But I must admit to a certain . . . I must confess that I cannot give you any clear interpretation of them. The typing here appears to have lost all system. From the end of page seven I cannot understand what the figures mean at all."

At the word *typing* a consciousness came over Alain: he could not tell whether it was shared by Xavier, who was silent now, apparently absorbed in the figures.

"Alain," said Xavier, again with that kind look, "you have been here a week, and you have never mentioned this business, this personal affair of mine: I appreciate it very much."

Alain was not going to let him go with that. "I will not pretend to misunderstand you," he said. "And I will not be such a hypocrite as to pretend that I am not brimming over with curiosity: the family have been filling me with strange tales these six months past."

"As long as that? You surprise me. I will not embarrass you by asking what they have said." There was a pause, and then Xavier said, "Shall we sit in the garden? It is stifling in here."

The garden was older than the house: its present form dated from the time when the Roussillon was a part of Spain. Spaniards had built the high, secret, enclosing wall; Spaniards had planted the enormous fig tree that filled the night with its animal scent and that was heaving the flagstones of the patio with a slow, desperate effort that had begun a hundred years before.

Alain and Xavier settled in long chairs on the second of the three descending terraces of the garden; they had brought the decanter, their glasses, the cigars, and the tourron by the light of the lamp, for it was black velvet night already; but now Alain had put it out for fear of the moths, and they sat in the starlight. He had thought of slipping upstairs for his dressing gown; but it would be madness to risk an interruption like that. Anyhow, it was not necessary: the heat rose still from the stones; the faint breeze was warm on his forehead; and from every tree the cicadas, drunk with warmth, strummed in a choir so uniform and unceasing that in five minutes it was inaudible.

"I have always envied you your profession, Alain," he said, after a long pause. "It must be a very real satisfaction to a man to know that what he is doing is good: to be able to say at the end of his life that he has spent his time accountably."

"It is a profession that can be easily idealized," said Alain, feeling disappointed and let down.

"But even so, surely there must be a deep — not exactly contentment, a sense of fulfillment rather, in using all the knowledge that a doctor has nowadays for unselfish ends? After all, there are so many activities, innumerable activities that a man can engage in and hardly know at the end of the count whether the balance is this way or that: negative trades, to say the best. With medicine at least you know that what you do is right."

"Yes, there is that aspect. And perhaps it would count for a great deal in the life of a man in general practice: he has opportunities enough, God knows. Though I have a strong feeling that once he starts pluming himself on his moral worth all his merit has left him. For myself, I don't know. The satisfaction in research is little more than the satisfaction of puzzle-solving raised to its highest degree. No: it *is* more than that. Just before I came away I finished a long series of experiments — brought them to a firm, distinct conclusion. The conclusion was that the vaccine on which I had been working was useless. But that in itself was an addition to the sum of knowledge: no other bacteriologist will ever have to spend a year of his life to solve that particular question again, and I remember the kind of self-approbation I experienced as I recorded my findings — a little priggish, perhaps, but a feeling that nothing else in the world could give you." He took a sip of his cognac, let it run slowly down his throat, and went on.

"Still, I think it is certainly a mistake to attribute very high motives or very high merit to researchers: it is true that the work is unselfish in that no immediate personal gain is in prospect (though the idea of personal glory is there quite often), but it is undertaken from interest in the subject, from a desire to *know,* regardless of values, and it is persisted in from obstinacy; laudable obstinacy, no doubt: but that is not the same thing as a clear-cut desire to serve one's fellow men.

"I don't wish to be extreme: I dare say that bacteriologists as a class do think very kindly of mankind as a whole when it occurs to them to think of it at all; but I think their guiding motive is curiosity rather than humanity. And I know that with regard to their fellow men as individuals they are neither much better nor much worse than the rest of the world: they certainly do not conspicuously overflow with love for their neighbors or their colleagues. And I am sure of this, that the popular idea of bacteriologists as wise white-coated angels yearning day and night is so much nonsense: many of them are disagreeable men, some not even of average intelligence. And any bacteriologist who gives countenance to this 'dedicated servant' notion is guilty of abominable cant. I hate cant."

"Yes. But cant and sentimentality aside, I still envy you. Compare medicine with the

121

law. In spite of everything that can be said against doctors, nobody has ever felt called upon to elaborate any long, sophistical argument to prove that medicine is an honorable calling: nor do they trouble to show that rich men have a better time than poor men. But it has been demonstrated over and over again, logically and conclusively, that the lawyer is all that is admirable and that poverty is in every way preferable to wealth. Yet the world's mind is unaltered: men still flee poverty and loathe lawyers."

"The concept of justice is very noble, surely?"

"Justice? Oh yes. The concept of cleanliness is very fine, too; but we do not cherish the emptiers of dustbins or the men who look after the sewers."

"You are determined to think ill of your trade, I find."

"Yes. It is a dirty, dirty business. I have never known anyone come in contact with the law, as winner, loser, or lawyer without taking some of the taint of it."

If I had studied psychology instead of bacteria, thought Alain, I might know what all this portends: if anyone had attacked the law on my last leave Xavier would have downed him with three or four sharp arguments and a dozen quotations: he would have been out of the house in a very short time, and he would never have been allowed in again.

Xavier was in a high, mounting state of nervous tension: all the time Alain had been talking he had noticed the end of Xavier's cigar glowing with his continual, restless drawing on it. Now the stump curved away in a long comet-flight that ended in a burst of sparks on the lower terrace, and at once Xavier lit another.

In the flare of the match his face stood out in exaggerated light and shade, gaunt, cadaverous, desperately unhappy.

"I'll tell you what it is, Alain," he said, in an odd, continuing voice, as if he had been speaking for some time. "Every day I see damnation just in front of me, and it terrifies me."

He was silent, and Alain, with the shock of surprise and embarrassment, could make no comment. This was delicate: but his continuing silence might have the air of repulsive, cold indifference — disinclination to speak so intimately. In a neutral voice he repeated the word damnation.

"Yes. Damnation."

"What do you mean by it?"

"Every sort of damnation. The devils-with-pitchforks damnation, the fiery hell, the icy hell, the silent hell of darkness and expectation, a waiting horror: everything. But specifically for me a kind of living death; damnation on two legs. Look here, Alain —" he was leaning forward in the urgency of his speech; Alain could feel his nearness — "do you know what I mean by the death of the soul?"

"No."

"I will tell you what I mean by the death of the soul. When you no longer have the power to love, when there is no stir of affection anywhere in your being, then your soul is dead. That is the death of your soul. Your soul is dead, and you are damned: you are dead walking, and you are in hell in your own body."

By day, in other surroundings, Alain might have discounted these big words: here, with the night around him, they moved him inexpressibly.

"What you say troubles me very much, Xavier," he said, after a long pause.

"Does it? It is a queer thing to spring on a man," he said, in a ghastly parody of his ordinary conversational voice, "but you must bear with me, Alain. You are the perfect confidant, you know: you will be thousands of miles away very soon, so I can speak with as much freedom as if you were a stranger in a train; yet I do not have to explain the background."

Alain made an assenting murmur.

"I suppose you think I am mad?"

"No. No, I don't think that at all. But I will say that I am surprised that your idea of damnation is so immediately real. You mean it literally, if I understand you rightly?"

"Of course I do. It is as real and immediate as this table. I mean nothing figurative: but of course it surprises you: with your nature and your manner of life I do not suppose that you have ever been face to face with it in all your days. I envy you, as I was saying just now." He was fiddling nervously with a match, grinding its stub on the table with a noise that set all Alain's teeth on edge. "What I do not understand," he said, snapping the match in two, "is how I come to be in this position. You may say that I have gained the whole world and lost my soul. Well, it is true that I have been a successful man: I have accomplished every material ambition that I set out to accomplish. I have not got a home or a family, but I have everything else. But all the time I have been honest; quixotically honest sometimes: I could have been a rich man ten years ago if I had chosen to be no more than a little supple.

125

"No; that does not make sense or justice. Sometimes I have thought that it is merely an affair of temperament — glandular secretion, isn't it? — and that it never was within my control. X has a sanguine temperament; Y has a melancholy temperament: one sees that every day. But to be damned for having a cold, phlegmatic nature — no, that is utterly repugnant to all doctrine or sense of equity.

"I wish I could point to some dramatic treachery on my part; some clear-cut gross offense against my own integrity, a crime even — I mean a legal crime — that would justify this present state. I could repent of that. But there is nothing. Nothing but a lifelong course of small, unloving selfishness; and how can a man repent for a million trifles, for a habit of mind? I do not know that you could call me an unusually selfish man now: I do not think so, for upon my word I am not very fond of myself. But I certainly was when I was an adolescent. I passed through my period of mysticism then. Even then I was frightened of damnation; and I was told (and thoroughly believed) that a man's first duty was to save his soul — his primary, imperative need. There may be a more selfish doctrine, but I do not think that I have ever met with one. No doubt I misinterpreted it, but it seemed to me to mean Save yourself, save yourself above all things, and let the rest go to the devil and to everlasting torment . . ."

ALAIN: Xavier, I can't hear you.

XAVIER: Oh, I beg your pardon. I was wandering — mumbling to myself about the origin of . . . I was trying to trace it back. But I will tell you, Alain, how it came to strike me first so terribly hard. You did not see much of Georgette: you were abroad nearly all the time of our marriage. If you had been here more you would have gathered that it was an unexceptionable marriage, reasonably happy in a quiet, uneventful way: and you would have thought that the sudden breaking of it in a few years would have been terribly painful for me — you did think so, indeed, to judge from the very kind letter you sent me. Well, it was not. The only pain I experienced was at the absence of my pain. The only emotion that I felt was irritation: I felt that she could have recovered if she had tried (poor thing, poor thing; she had little cause to try) and that now I should be exposed to all the fuss of the burial, and then to the inconvenience of living without someone to look after the house and the child. No: that was not the only emotion; but it was the only unpleasant emotion. I also felt relief, and it was not without a real pleasure that I looked forward — even at that moment, sitting by her bed — to my quiet, solitary evenings again, and my walks in the country; the one without the consciousness of someone sitting there being quiet, and the other without having to walk slowly or choose suitable, easy paths.

I cannot tell you how it shocked me to find that these were my feelings. It was a horrible shock. It could be said, in mitigation, that the marriage had not been a romantic one in the first place, not on my side, that is: the proposals were made by her father, as you know. And it could be said that on the physical side the marriage was not successful. But with every conceivable allowance it remained a horrible shock to look into my mind and find that it was so callous; so hideously callous. After all, nothing could change the fact that we had lived in the closest intimacy for years, that she had been a true and loving wife to me as far as she could, and that she was Dédé's mother. That was the first time in my life that I pretended to an emotion that I did not feel, and the first time that I was ashamed of not feeling it. Before, I had plumed myself on my intellectual honesty; I had thought well of myself for not expressing the glib, insincere sentiments that flow on every occasion. When Dédé was born, for example, I was disappointed to find that I did not experience those raptures that are supposed to arise in a man seeing his wife with their first child. I did not find the child a sympathetic object, but indeed rather a disgusting one; and the sight of Georgette, radiant, worn and animal, suckling it, made my gorge rise. So then I made no pretense at conventional transports: but now, now I mimed the bereaved husband. It was not only that I felt the utter indecency of my indifference: it was that the indifference frightened, terrified me, and by a mechanical, superstitious mourning I tried to avert the omen.

It was a terrible shock. I keep repeating that, because every day the shock was repeated in me: I would wake up in the morning, alone in my room, remember that Georgette was not there, and realize once again that I did not care at all.

It was then that I began to look forward and back with a new eye. The detachment that I had been proud of was terribly suspect now. Before, I had seen nothing wrong in not professing emotions that I did not feel; and, to speak candidly, I had supposed that a great proportion of the professions made in the world were false: now, it suddenly came upon me that I had been wrong in not feeling that somewhere back along the line was the beginning of death, and that it was the world that was right and not myself — that it was not the world that was hypocritical but I who was unfeeling. That 'unfeeling' is a small enough word, God knows: but what an infinity there is in it.

It was in this careful, horrified looking back that I tried to trace out the progression of this — what? emotional paralysis, spiritual palsy? Creeping leprosy of the soul, deadening.

Bombast, bombast, you say: but sitting by that dead pale body it did not seem bombast to me. Nor did it ever seem bombast to me afterward. Perhaps it is wrong to say that nothing has so much importance to a man as the deliberate saving of his soul: but I am certain, my God I am certain, that nothing is so important as the knowing loss of it.

— Xavier stopped, and scraped miserably about the table for the cigars. Alain guided the box to his hand, and in a minute the unhappy voice began again.

XAVIER: I began by asking myself what proof I had that the emotions that one sees all round one had any real existence. If they did not exist in me, did they in anybody else? It was difficult to bring much concrete evidence for the existence of affection and loving-kindness: they express themselves so much more in the general air of men and women — looks, intonation — rather than in isolated, distinct actions. And then with actions, the possibility of misinterpretation is so . . . but I need not elaborate. It was clear that these feelings did exist: I could see them most plainly in the writing that I admired and in the actions of men I respected — not the emotions themselves, but the continual reflection of them. It was obvious that not all these people were lying: a man accustomed to weighing evidence is quick at detecting a lie. And if I needed corroboration I had only to look back far enough to find them known and proved in myself. When I was a really small boy I loved my stepmother, you know, and when they quarrelled I hated my father. I loved her, and I thought about things for her and how when I grew up I would do this, that, and the other to give her pleasure: and when they took her away I was so desolate — desolate. But even then, at its tenderest, my power of affection must have been of a feeble growth, for when they told me that she had died there, I was more concerned with acting, tasting the importance of tragedy, than with genuine regret. Yet it is unfair to say that: I was only a very little boy, and she had been in that place a year — a year is such a long period in a child's life.

But when I looked to find the beginning, I could find nothing clear or distinct. Somehow between that time and this I had turned from a normal affectionate child, or at least a child loving enough to hate fiercely for another's sake, into a man so abnormal that he had not the power to feel any sorrow for his wife's death. And not only that: terribly startled by what was, in all conscience, a striking instance of hardness, I looked into the rest of my feelings: there was no affection there, none at all. And as a consequence there was no true charity. That indeed was the crux: no charity. Since I had been a man I had never performed one solitary act of charity.

Some time after the funeral I went to see the curé: it was Father Sabatier then. I was still in a very agitated frame of mind, and I did not succeed in making myself clear to him. I do not think I could have made him understand at any time: he was a good man, a very good man indeed, as you know, but he did not have a clear intelligence and he had always been in awe of us — of Aunt Margot and me. He was more concerned to reassure and comfort me than to show me any spiritual remedy: he spent himself in proving that I was *not* halfway down a gulf, or worse; he did not attempt to show me a way out. To set my mind at rest he catalogued my virtues, abstemiousness, chastity, justice, prudence, fortitude, almsgiving. I tried to show him that what good actions he could mention were insignificant because they had no real kindness in them — mere good works, acknowledgments of an exterior virtue, done from a sense of what was due, what was right. He swam into the deep water of good works, floundered — he was never strong in doctrine — but came out to assure me that if I continued in my duties and prayed for grace I should be quite all right. He was quite exhausted, poor good old man, and in the end I left him alone.

— There was a long, reflective pause, then Xavier's deep voice continued, more equably now, more equably, and still the cicadas thrummed in all the trees.

The Pleiades had risen now: Alain could see them all, all but the last, a cluster above the fig tree. In the beginning he had listened closely to Xavier, closely, anxiously, sitting upright and with his mind stretched to hear and understand everything: the urgency of Xavier's voice had required that reaction, the closeness, the assenting grunt, the head nodded in the darkness. But for a long while now he had been sitting back, lying back, in his chair: Xavier's voice had settled into a steady, even flow that made no demands; and Alain was no longer listening with the top of his mind. All that was said he heard and understood. But he was not listening, listening to catch each word; now the sense flowed in at his ears — he could reconstruct the whole — but now his easier mind could also run to and fro, combining what Xavier had said with what he knew, assessing the knowledge he had and the continual stream of addition to it; and now his half-conscious observing faculty was free again. It had been so since his cousin had begun on works without faith, a long and intricate subject that had nothing to say to Dr. Roig. He recorded the fact that points of fine theology were of strong and immediate importance to Xavier, and that Xavier seemed to feel that religion and the law could both be logically discussed and reasoned upon with the same reference to precedent. But in this chain of reasoning Alain took no part, not even that of a silent follower: he formed from it a picture of Xavier's mind — a picture made up of small impressions, the repetition of "Jansenists," the approving tone in which Pascal's name was mentioned, the citation of many, many writers unknown to

Alain, but which reflected a wide and anxious reading. With that part of his attention which was at liberty he watched the progress of the stars.

It had been the great ball of Jupiter first: when they had sat down the star was already high, so brilliant that it had a halo and so large that it was not a point in the sky but a disk. When they had sat down — it was after they had put out the lamp — Alain had half-consciously fixed the star in his mind: "There is Jupiter: how huge and brilliant." But unnoticed in the first spate of talk Jupiter had climbed to the zenith, still in front of the Dog Star, whose light it eclipsed, and had traveled down the sky, far down to the right. It was when Xavier was talking of his father that Alain realized that the planet was gone, hidden behind the straight trunk of the palm tree on the declining west, lighting it from behind with a last gentle refulgence, and that the Dog Star, brilliant now, was halfway down to setting.

Betelgeuse and Aldebaran: he watched them pass through the motionless, penetrable eucalyptus, branch by branch, lost and reappearing through the leaves; the continual curving sweep of stars. The progress of the stars and the run of his cousin's voice: the time came when Alain, lying right

135

back, deep in his chair, seemed hardly to possess a body, to be no more than a mind in a place, absorbing these two processions, relating and enfolding them.

And then something was wrong, something was out of joint, as if the cicadas had stopped, or the night had suddenly grown cold. Sunk, or rather floating there, he had constructed the sense of what he heard with a lag of perhaps two or three sentences — a lag made longer sometimes when his own glosses on the unfolding text, footnotes, references, grew long and complex. He heard all that the steady voice said, but not what it was saying; so now, uncomfortably aware of a pause, an expectant pause, a question that had been repeated, something that demanded his participation, he forced himself to the surface, trying to hasten his mind's process, catch up, understand. What was it? Xavier had been developing an idea about literal unbelief, figurative acceptance — necessity for the rejection of Heaven by the unbeliever but complete acceptance of Hell. Yes: but the last sentences, the immediate question?

"What do you believe, Alain?" he said again.

Alain was furious. Not only had be been wrenched brutally out of a wonderfully comfortable state, but he was being attacked with a question that should never have been asked. No no, he said (but not aloud), that will not do: I am not going to take off my clothes just because you have done so: there was no compact. You have not bought the right to a truthful answer: your truth has not bought it. Sincerity is not to be bought: it is given, if it comes at all — given or inflicted. And really, you cannot invade a man's privacy like that.

"Well, it is difficult to say," he replied at last, uncomfortably, but with sufficient earnestness (a half-hypocrisy licensed by the unwarranted question) not to appear evasive — not to repel. "Credo in unum Deum . . ." his voice trailed away.

In the long pause that followed Alain thought that it was finished now, that this unfortunate question and answer had been the stone that puts the birds to flight: but when Xavier spoke again it was obvious that he had hardly listened to the reply, that the argument had continued in his own silence. Now he took it up again, several stages along in the development, in almost the same voice, as if there had been no break at all.

But the break had been long and painful for Alain: the abrupt, violent change from

137

audience to performer could not be quickly reversed. It was not until Sirius touched the first of the western palm fronds that he had sunk back to something near his former depth. Now Xavier was returning toward an account of his progress: he had almost finished with his more general, imprecise way of speaking, but some fragments of what he had been saying floated in Alain's head, waiting to be fixed if they were significant. "I am not a Communist (God forbid), but nothing I have ever heard of them has made me respect them half so much as their belief that it is indecent for a man to live to himself alone, to direct most of his energies to the acquisition of a comfortable home for himself and a safe future. I understand that this is a universal conviction, a basic social convention in Russia, so penetrating that even discontented, anti-Communist refugees reaching our world are shocked by the open avowal of selfishness here, as if by indecent exposure. However corrupt their practice may be, and however wicked their designs, a society that has that teaching surpasses ours, as a true *society,* as much as the living, every-day-of-the-week faith of the Middle Ages surpassed our moribund Sundays-only half-belief." "Love your neighbor as yourself is not enough, nothing like enough, if you have a deep, well-founded dislike of yourself." "Even if I did flatter myself into believing that I had half these virtues, or even all of them, it would make no difference: they are the Stoic virtues, the natural virtues, not the Christian virtues. Valuable, perhaps, in a general way — at least you despise a man *without* them — valuable perhaps, but not valid for me. Not valid, not relevant." (With the former pain and urgency renewed.) "Not valid, any more than giving away money without good will — alms without kindness."

But those were things that had been said. Now Alain, while he still kept them on one side for arrangement, was thinking "He is a clear-sighted man: has he never realized how much he has indulged his superiority and his irritable nature?" And at once, as if it were Alain who was guiding the run of words, Xavier branched off and said, "How can you ever tell if another man is suffering more pain than you, or less? So that in the one case it is heroic in him not to cry out, and in the second cowardly even to wince? You cannot tell: you can only suppose. In the same way I cannot tell whether in fact I have a more irascible nature than others, really feel a higher degree of irritation, or merely yield more easily to the temptation, grow hot and angry when other men exercise more self-control. But I have always supposed that that was the case, and that those who behaved better were only more phlegmatic: it was a comfortable doctrine; it diminished the fault, and I must say that even now I believe it to be more true than false.

"But however that may be, I have always noticed that in general small and large vexations, but especially trivial ones, often make me so furious that I have to put my hands in my pockets and turn away not to make a fool of myself — and this when other men remain perfectly unmoved. I used to be secretly a little flattered at my sensitivity and at my ability to cover it; and although I was aware, very clearly aware, that a degree of sensitivity that causes a man to pass perhaps a third of his lifetime in a state of intense, though disguised, irritation is no very welcome gift, yet it was not until this time that I came to suspect it as a wickedness, a thing that corrupts the very source of affection.

"I resolved (oh with such a heart-felt resolution) not merely to curb my impatience — I had done that all my life — but to prevent its arising: and I resolved to cultivate a loving indulgence for my fellows, particularly those who vexed me. I knew that it would to a large extent be artificial at first, but I hoped that the quality would grow behind the pretense, like the face behind the mask in the story.

"It was not with enthusiasm that I began on this new course: enthusiasm has a sound of warmth and pleasure. No: it was more as a man seizes upon a lifeline: he does not seize it with enthusiasm but with — what? Not desperation, for there is hope. The word escapes me: but it was with this same kind of feeling that I began.

"During Georgette's long illness Dédé had lived with Aunt Marinette, and they suggested that he should stay with them. There was a good deal to be said for the arrangement. I was very busy at that time, and in many ways Aunt Marinette's house was more suitable for a child. But I thought it better to have him at home: he was backward, I knew, and Aunt Marinette, though kind, was not an ideal person to bring up a boy.

"I would find time, cost what it might, to see to his education, and I would bring him up with loving-kindness and indulgence tempered with good sense. He was my own son, my only son, and if I could not find a tenderness in my heart even for him, then

141

indeed I was a monster. I knew that I was not fond of children in general, but this was not anybody's child, it was my own, and I had little doubt of the success of my scheme.

"At the same time I bought a dog. Here again I knew that I was not what is called good with dogs, but I felt convinced that good will and common sense would make up for that.

"I was younger then. I should be less sanguine now, and now perhaps I might foresee disaster in such schemes: for disasters they both were, disasters.

"An unskillful man is generally unlucky as well, don't you find? A man who is not a good driver is run into through no fault of his own, has a puncture every time he goes out, or some bizarre misadventure happens to him when it would not happen to anyone else. It was the same with me: I happened to fall on the child and the dog for whom ordinary, kind treatment was not suitable.

"I will tell you about the dog first. It was a young liver-colored dog with a pink nose that Côme found for me. I knew nothing of these things, and asked him: I had to bow to his choice, of course, but it seemed a poor-looking creature to me. I suppose that it is very usual to trust a man in his trade although you know him to be a fool in other respects: anyhow, although I always considered Côme a lecherous half-wit (and still do) I thought that as he was always hunting or shooting with the aid of dogs, always among them, he would act intelligently in this instance. However, the dog proved to be as much a fool as Côme. It was said to be house-trained, but it was not, and that was a wearisome business. It was worse than that, for it started everything off on the wrong foot — it started with distaste and unkind feelings. It was a dog, I should have said, with overabundant energy and spirits, and at first it overflowed with indiscriminate, meaningless affection to such an extent that it was a nuisance. Unless it was restrained all the time it would break out into noisy excesses, grow overexcited and hysterical, take the wildest liberties. All the time it had to be checked or there was no peace, no possibility of obedience: kindness after restraint sent it off its head.

"It was unfortunate that the first beating I ever gave the dog had a wonderful effect: it encouraged me to think for a long time that that was the best way of teaching it. There was so much that it had to be taught, so much that ordinary dogs seem to know intuitively — or perhaps I am wrong in saying that; perhaps I am judging from trained dogs. This dog — its name was Pedro — had to be taught not to stray, roaming the streets and picking in the dustbins, not to make filthy messes in this house and in other people's, not to jump up, not to tear up plants in the garden, not to dig holes — oh, an infinity of lessons: and it learned very slowly and stupidly, if at all. To the end it could never be stopped barking at everybody or straying and haunting the rubbish heaps with the village curs. It had a great deal of cur in it, although it was said to be so well bred: it was quarrelsome, aggressive with other dogs, but the moment they showed their teeth, Pedro would run howling. Oh, it was a disaster, that dog. Yet there was a time when I did have a certain weak fondness for it: even the worst dog has some pretty ways when it is young. Occasionally, too, it would try to learn something and I would be pleased with it. But then fatally the next moment it would do something maddening and I would have to speak to it sharply — unless it was instantly checked it would continue to behave badly; it was a dog that took advantage at once of weakness or indulgence. I would speak to it sharply and it would start to cower. That cowering, crawling on its belly: I believe it feigned half the time. Certainly it did it more when we were out than at home. I would call it: it would not come — it was busy eating filth. I would call it sharply, go back toward it, and at once it would start this creeping off, flat on the ground, leaving a piddling stream behind it, as if I habitually lashed it to bloody insensibility. I could never teach it to come, or to stay reliably in to heel; and once it was out of arm's reach it would chase sheep, goats, hens, anything that would run: so it was no companion on a walk. Nor could I ever teach it not to hang about the kitchen day and night: so in the end, when it appeared that I had reduced it to a cowering, hysterical, incontinent, useless cur, and when it was clear that it had no affection for me whatever, only a guilty desire to get out of my way, I gave in, let it go into the kitchen for good (they had always encouraged it) and there it remained, grossly bloated, an ill-conditioned bawler to the end of its days, when it bit the woman who had fed it for nine years, bit her viciously, and she smashed in its skull with a pestle.

"Well, the parallel disaster of the child was not so dramatic; and it is not complete. Obviously, there is no comparison in the importance of the two (though it was surprising how that dog rested on my heart, for years and years) and obviously my hopes and efforts were far, far more important.

"I listed the bad qualities of that dog so much at random that I do not know whether I conveyed the chief fault — the chief fault from my point of view — that it was not to be taught by kindness, that kindness was not the key to its nature.

"It was the same with Dédé. He had been a long time with Aunt Marinette, as I have said, and for a long while before that I had not occupied myself with him very much: a man is out of place in a nursery. So he came home almost a stranger to me, and I was very much surprised to find what a nasty little boy he was. I do not suppose that I should ever have fully discovered it if it had not been for my new, imposed attitude of mild tolerance, and my attempt at helping with his education. He had been very badly spoilt in his babyhood, and he had just come from being abominably spoilt by Aunt Marinette, so a great deal of his nastiness was not to be imputed to him. In passing, I could say a great deal about women and the bringing-up of children, but I will not: I will just observe that I have met with precious few in the course of my life who were fit to be trusted with such a charge. Aunt Marinette was not one of them. But even making every allowance, he was a disagreeable little boy in his own right. No doubt I had an exalted idea of what my son ought to be like, far too exalted, but still I think at bottom I should have been satisfied with a manly boy, even if he had been affected, untruthful, hypocritical, unaffectionate, cruel, and of course grossly ill-mannered and undisciplined. During that first period I was able to look at him very thoroughly: believe me, Alain, a parent's eye is not so blind as they say; when it is searching as desperately as mine was, it is as keen as an enemy's. I looked into his shallow little soul, and I found that in addition to all those disagreeable qualities it had an epicene namby-pambyness that filled me with despair — it seemed to go through and through him, to be basic and ineradicable.

"Oh, those horrible lessons. I could not, even by the greatest economy of my working time, make more than two hours a day for him, one in the morning and one in the evening. It was a short enough time measured by the clock, but how it dragged on and on and on. At first, when he found that I was not to be feared, he would mince about showing off like a confident little ape, or he would give a performance of himself in the role of the arch, winning little boy, so quaint: it was a shocking indictment of the people he had been with, for it had evidently taken them in and pleased them. You know the kind of thing, head on one side, simper, saccharine expression. He would do this showing off for me alone — when there was no other audience but myself, I mean. Any child is liable to show off when there are many people there, particularly strangers, but surely it is very rare for a child to do it perpetually, even when there is only one person? It means that there is no possibility of any companionship, no human contact at all. And the ghastly thing was that what he wished to imitate was not an older child but a *younger* one. I cannot tell you how distasteful it was. However, I put it down to his spoiling, tried not to blame him for it, tried to wean him from it by whatever gentle means I could conceive, tried hard to like him in spite of it, and tried, quite vainly, to win his liking and his confidence.

"He was very backward, as I said, very backward indeed; and after a while I began to grow seriously worried. If I did not change my methods I should never be able to get him on so that he could compete with boys of his own age. Indulgence had not worked so far, and we did not have unlimited time in which to see whether it would ever work. In order to get him to learn at all it was essential to take a very different tone: and that I did. It was the pity of the world that there was no affection in him: if there had been, he might have tried to learn a little to please me. But he never did that.

"I had sat so long at that table with a fixed, tolerant smile, watching him go through his paces — you would not know, Alain, not having a child, how horribly wounding it is to see a thoroughly affected boy, a boy corrupted through and through with affectation so that there is no true boy left at all, no core of genuine being left inside the mass of affectation, how wounding it is to realize that that has happened to any child, and how triply wounding when that child is yours, part of you, identified with you — your continuity, in fact, your own physical survival and renewal. And it is all the more intimately, personally wounding — wounding to one's vanity, if you like, but *wounding* — because in the child you see horrible glimpses of yourself. There is no forgetting that you are essentially implicated. I did not see very much — one is not well acquainted with one's own superficial peculiarities, so I dare say that a good deal escaped my attention — but what I did see was the cruelest caricature; a very ingenious enemy could not have hurt me more. There was much more of his mother paraded before me: but never once did I catch any hint of her amiable qualities. Her weakness, silliness, and dishonesty of mind were there, as clearly reproduced as her long, pale, chinless face and pale, uncolored hair, but I could never find a trace of her loving heart, her earnest desire to please, her patience, or her generally kind and affectionate nature. She had been fond of birds — the fondness that expresses itself by shutting them up in cages for the term of their lives, but a genuine feeling of kindness nevertheless. Dédé with a living bird or any small creature in his power was a sight to make your heart sick. It is a natural childish phase, they say; but to *that* extent . . .

"However, I am wandering. It was a positive relief, I say, after a long stretch of this dreary exhibition, a positive relief to snap out a few hard words in a natural voice and put an end to it. I knew very well that it went on out of sight, but at least I did not see it so much, and that was something. My chief concern now was to get the boy on, bring him up to the standard for his age. I knew that Soulier was not doing anything with him — Soulier came to teach him during the daytime — and probably could not; and I felt very strongly that if I did not bring him on myself he would remain one of those permanently backward louts like Marcelin Py. If he went to school at all it would be to remain at the bottom of everything, the buffoon of the class — every class has one — until he was superannuated, a hairy hobbledehoy only capable of running after servant girls and dressing up. Though on second thoughts, Dédé would never run after servant girls; he is too lymphatic, and far too much of a snob. We were still at the elements, reading, writing, and arithmetic. For the first long weeks and months there was almost no progress at all: it was not until I began to impose some degree of discipline that he began to use his brain at all, and even then he was so unused to using it, and still so preoccupied with being the quaint wonderchild, that progress was agonizingly slow.

"This second, intermediate phase, did not last long. He understood that I would no longer stand gross foolery and idleness during lessons, and he very quickly found new ways of not working and, seeing that there was open hostility now, ways of irritating me. It was remarkable, really, to see how well a boy who was in most ways stupid and insensitive, could pick on just those affectations and cunning tricks that were best suited to vex. He had a damned lisp, quite fictitious, and a way of drawing out his words when he was reading that made me long to knock the book out of his hand — he knew it very well, too, and he knew that I would not do it. But worse than the lisp was the invincible conviction that it was quaint to be stupid. We would come up against a difficult word in reading: I would lead him toward its pronunciation by analogies, half a dozen of them: he would get them all right, and there I would be, all tense with the desire to plant the idea into his head, and tense with desire to hear the right answer; and at the end of the chain of analogies, while my lips would be forming the right word for him, he would cock his head on one side, utter his 'silvery laugh' ha, ha, ha, ha, and say the word wrongly, with a complacent smirk on his pasty face.

"It was bound to end the way it did. One day he tried me too far and I gave him a clout that did my heart good. It was a great relief, but it was the beginning of the end. I think now that however tried he may be, a man should not knock children about. It had an excellent effect at the time: that day and the next we made more progress than we had for weeks. Then the stimulus wore off, and he relapsed until I clouted him again — another spurt, but shorter this time: and so it went on, from bad to worse. It was true that he learned a good deal: but at what a price. It was formal beatings now, and they were more and more frequent. There never was a lesson without tears and shouting; yet although he loathed a bad day and dreaded a beating, still he would keep to his affectations: to the very end he would lisp, he would feign to misunderstand and he would trail out his words, he would mumble when he was reading aloud, and he would push me to the very edge of final exasperation with a truly incredible persistence.

"Well, I beat him and I knocked him about. I justified myself in many ways — Solomon, my father's example: he beat me, you know, with no justification at all, or on a trumped-up charge neither of us believed in, and yet it never did me much harm. But there was the necessity for justification; and although there was justification at hand (in passing, I may say now that I do not think any other method could have got him up to the required standard in time) it could not outweigh the fact that I was struck with shame on the rare occasions when someone came into the room while I was in full cry, or passed by the window. I had suffered so much from bullying — from mental assault much more than from beating, which I took as it came — so much from the atmosphere of domestic tyranny when I was a boy, that I had a very particular loathing for the character of a tyrant: and yet here I was, ranting and bawling at the boy . . . My motive was good: and I did not try to batter down his self-respect, nor humiliate him; but to an outsider the difference between my conduct and a tyrant's would have needed a good deal of explanation. There *was* an essential difference; but there was also a strong, if superficial, similarity, and I felt it keenly.

"Then I went too far. Repeated exasperation made me more irritable than ever: the very sight of that beastly yellow spelling book made my temper seethe, and lessons began in a hopeless atmosphere. And repeated punishment made Dédé stupid — a superadded stupidity — and weakened his resistance so that he took to crying with no direct cause. Yet still that child remained very nearly as affected as he was at the beginning. In the last months, quite sickened by the wreck that I had made of it, I swore to God that I would never touch him again; and I never did. His progress stopped almost completely, the lisp came back to its full extent and with it the head-on-one-side smirk when he made some conscious little-boy remark.

"But I did not care: he was ready for school, and right heartily glad I was when I could pack him off — as glad as he was to go, because he never trusted me not to break out again. Poor little boy: I was so sorry for him when he was not there; and then the moment he appeared I longed for him to go away.

"I tell you Alain, there is a great deal said and written nowadays about parents and children — how badly parents bring their children up, how they domineer, tyrannize, maltreat them psychologically. But there is precious little said on the parents' side; nobody speaks of the oppression of the parents by the children. That little boy fairly poisoned my days; he baited me with the cunning and persistence of a grown woman, and he felt more malice than I should ever have supposed a child could contain. Every second novel nowadays has a sensitive young man who was badly used by his father: I would cut a pretty figure in a book like that — I might almost have been made for the role of the villain. But believe me, there is a great deal, a very great deal, to be said on the other side.

"I used to dislike my father. I still do. But

now I remember how often I irritated him, and now I know far more clearly the standards by which his mind worked; I know the corrupting influence of unchecked power and continual vexation, and I dislike him much less. Perhaps it is that in justifying myself I must to some extent justify my father; but it is more than that, I am sure. But that aside: what I wanted to show was not merely that my attempt at loving, liking, feeling affection for these two beings was a complete failure (and much the same applies to my resolution of more general benevolence) but that in the event it was bound to be so. In the case of Dédé it was impossible to like him and remain honest: no clear-thinking man could know that child as I knew him and still find anything likable there. And after all, the animal approach of 'my son, therefore excellent' is not worth much, is it?

"Now that was a terribly long digression. I am boring you cruelly, I know, Alain, cruelly and unwarrantably; but you will bear with me this once. It is a good action."

Poor shrunken Alain. He had been comfortable, warm, contemplative once; but that was years ago. Now he was hunched over his cold and trembling stomach, and now even the stars he watched with his dull, extinguished eye were pale. Pale? Yes, they were pale in the lightening sky: there was still night down there where they were setting, but on the left hand there was the green of dawn. And now Xavier was asking him to bear with him. Alain made the inarticulate consenting noise that civility required — "Oh, not at all. By all means. Please go on."

In the fig tree a bird was singing. His eyes, tired and flickering though they were, could see the color of the leaves now. It was wonderful how the light increased, a duck's-egg green that spread right over the bowl of the sky, ethereally pure colors, then the real blue down there. For a moment there was day on the one hand and night on the other, balanced, with the vast luminous dayspring in between. then the day won. It was an event of huge importance: birds sang: the air moved — a dry rustle from the palm fronds — and in the sky flamingo banners took form and color. Pointing up into the luminous air there came the rays of the sun; the eastern horizon, the taut line of the sea, glowed incandescent; the rays swept lower, touched the stony mountain on the right, crept down, and then the rim of the sun heaved up, the first white, blinding glimpse of the day.

Xavier would not acknowledge the dawn. The day would oblige him to turn and look at Alain, which he could not do and continue: and yet he had so much still unsaid. He wished to make it clear, *clear:* a logical exposition of the whole case, if he could accomplish it, would be of such enormous value, a corroboration for himself, a clearing of his mind.

He must hurry: he had wanted to elaborate so many points that he must now skim over if ever he was to have the time to resume all the lines of great importance and present a clear summing-up. Alain gazed hopefully at the sun: soon its rays would be down in the garden, bringing warmth, and perhaps they would thaw the rigid cold out of him; it seemed unlikely that anything could ever do that again, but perhaps the sun might succeed; if it did, he could bear anything.

"So, do you see," Xavier was saying urgently, "I saw the whole pattern reforming; myself dying, Dédé's uneasy delight and then a little later, when more sense or experience had come to him, the first chilling doubt in his mind about his own decency, followed by the same catastrophic self-examination, or by an equally catastrophic lack of it: in either case, the consciousness, more or less acute, according to his powers of self-deception, the consciousness and certainty of death."

The sun was on him now, but still he shivered: there was warmth in the sun, however.

"But still, but still," Xavier cried passionately, "this, all this, is only my exordium. What I wanted to show you, what I have failed to show you, except in a dull, imperfect fashion, was the state of a mind with no power of affection left in it, and the state of that mind when it is certain that the consequence of that paralysis is death. That self-induced or inflicted paralysis, or both, that wicked and blasphemous paralysis of love, whose consequence is death of the soul in life and damnation after it to all eternity. Damnation as certain as *that*," he cried, hitting the table savagely. "Think of that mind, man, try for God's sake to enter it, and then say what that mind must feel when for the first time it is conscious of a spontaneous jet of affection, the new, saving, healing, vivifying, humanizing feeling of love. . . . What? What is it? Oh what is it in God's name, woman?"

Unmoved by the trembling harshness in her master's voice or his lined and drawn face jerked over on one shoulder toward her, she said righteously, "Seeing that you and Monsieur Alain were up already, I thought you would like your coffee brought out on to the terrace."

Chapter Five

The conversation could never recover from this brutal interruption. Xavier, sitting there silent and haunted, was obviously in the throes of a violent reaction: he had been wound up emotionally to the highest pitch and now the tension was released so suddenly that his spirits were all abroad. Alain, a little revived by two bowls of scalding coffee, thought of the simile of a man running at great speed and tripping, being hurled flat by some trifling obstacle that would never have hindered him at all but for the speed of his running. After a moment's thought he repeated the idea to Xavier. He must contribute something, he felt, toward making the atmosphere possible again, and any remark about the freshness of the air, the color of the sky, anything obviously alien to the subject, would be dreadfully discordant. But for the moment Xavier could not respond. "Yes, yes," he said, in a vague tone; then, imperiously, "More coffee?" He turned his face to Alain as he spoke; there was an inimical look upon it, and his next remark, "Shall we go down and watch the boats come in?" had no friendliness, and the words came out unnaturally.

There was nothing in the world that Alain wanted more than a hot bath, hot enough to send the warmth right into the middle of his body, and then the cool sheets of his bed, the firm but yielding pillow. He would have given in to Xavier's suggestion not many years before, but now he said, "No. I'm going to have one more bowl of coffee, then I'm going to bed. A bath first."

Xavier sniffed. "You're very welcome to a bath, but it is not worth going to bed. We have an appointment with Cazeilles at eleven."

"Who?"

"Cazeilles. Aspullabalitris."

"Oh, him. Couldn't we put him off?"

"You will feel perfectly well after a cold shower," said Xavier. He lit a cigarette, and Alain noticed that his hand, the hand holding the match, was trembling so much that it took him as long to light it as a cigar. "Very well," he said internally, "if you wish to regain your composure by domineering a little, I have nothing to say. But it is not very amiable."

Xavier went in while Alain was still drinking his coffee, and out there in the garden Alain could hear his loud, rather harsh voice in the house: he was complaining of something.

"Poor devil," said Alain.

And "Poor devil," he said, lowering his tired body into the deep luxury of the bath.

He had been profoundly moved, and although the strength and the shock of his first impression were now overlaid with tiredness, still under the trivialities of his current thoughts there remained a great quantity of amazement at this revelation of an unknown, unsuspected man, and a very great deal of pity for him. "And yet," he thought uneasily, after a long while, "does he not overestimate the amount of affection there is in the world?"

The servants were clanging up and down the passage now: he had stayed far too long in the water, and his hands were wrinkled like a washerwoman's.

"I wonder how much every man's heart hardens as he goes farther and farther from his boyhood," he thought, sitting on the edge of the bath while the water sucked and gurgled away, and he thought of the tenderness of his own heart once, and how, a very young man new to the East, he had wept so bitterly for Li Fu-jen, the daughter of the scholar of Mô.

"And yet," he said to himself, "it is less sympathy for Xavier himself than consternation or dismay at the existence of the situation, and sorrow that *any* man, rather than one specific man, should be in it."

They had already got into his room and they were sweeping and banging the windows when he went back for his razor: it took him five minutes to get them out, and then they went straight into the bathroom. How very unlike Chinese servants, he thought, running his hand over his cheek; however, it did not really matter.

Now that they had just done the room it seemed indecent to get into the bed, so he lay on it for a while. He was tired, but the pints of strong coffee and his bath had done away with sleep, and when he heard the irregular staccato of a typewriter somewhere in the house his mind went running along on that line.

So there she was in the house, typing. Yes, it was today that she was due back: Aunt Margot had told him, but he had forgotten. Unless it was that miserable old clerk. No, he could never manage more than one finger at a time, and this was the trained, machine-gun stutter of an expert. It was the young woman, without any doubt. He felt a strong curiosity to see her, and when he had lain there a little longer, thinking, he dressed and went downstairs. He had taken the decision, remarkable for him, to walk into the room where she was without any disguise or pretense. It was not delicate, not delicate at all, he had reflected, but every sort of misconduct has two sides at least — adultery is a heinous tragedy to the cuckold, but dashing and doggish to the seducer; prying is ignoble and sordid to the detached observer, but a peccadillo, quite permissible to the curious.

The decision wavered, however, when he stood outside the door: it was really too gross to burst in like that. And as he stood, hesitating before going away, the door opened, and Xavier was there, looking unnaturally tall with the light behind him.

"Ah, there you are, Alain," he said. "I was about to come — I should like you to meet Madeleine."

There was the triangle; Xavier at the apex, Madeleine on his left at the bottom of the room, Alain on his right still by the door; and the lines of consciousness and regard made the three busy sides of the figure. Xavier was the most self-possessed; precise, cold-showered, well-shaved; and he was in his own room. But even Xavier was in some degree of flurry, and there was a hint of color in his gray face, a certain empressement in his movements that showed he was not entirely at his ease. Alain, confused by having the door suddenly opened on him, felt as uncomfortable as if he had been found listening at the keyhole. This was not the girl he had seen in the town some time ago, but another, and far, far prettier; she was perhaps the prettiest creature he had ever seen, for a European, and now that she was standing up at her desk, a little awkwardly because of the nearness of her chair to the desk, and a little awkwardly because she was not sure whether she should stand up, a blush mounted in her cheeks: she looked so agreeable, so very agreeable, that Alain smiled with pleasure, and when they shook hands he said, with unwonted cordiality, that it was a long time since he had seen her. It was an inept remark, so far as the words were concerned, and untrue in suggestion, but it conveyed, and it was meant to convey, civility, kindliness, and even approbation.

For a moment nobody said anything more, and in the silence Alain regretted his bristly face: his unshaved jaw rasped under his hand. Then Xavier said that Madeleine

166

was very kindly finishing the report on Aspullabalitris' vineyard; she was now on the last page, and from what was already done Alain would be able to judge the effect of the new culture. He passed the sheets to Alain and said, "I thought you would like to see this before we go up there."

"Yes, indeed," said Alain, sitting down. "Thank you very much." He glanced down the column of figures, but he could hardly bring his attention to bear, and before he had grasped even their general significance Xavier spoke again. He was standing behind Madeleine as she finished her page, and he said, "I really do not know how we managed with these tabulated accounts before Madeleine was kind enough to come and help us out." As he spoke he put his hand on her shoulder, and Alain saw the embarrassed smile on her face turn to something a little more forced, a smile still, held by politeness, but more artificial now and forced; and he saw her shoulder give to avoid the contact. It moved only enough to hint at the gesture of withdrawal before she held it still, but even that very small movement was enough to put an unnaturalness into the poise of her body, and now she had an air of constraint, almost of fixed rigidity.

Alain looked at Xavier, but there seemed

to be no awareness on his face: no, he went on talking about the benefits of office machinery, with an animated, unusually cheerful expression; and apparently without thinking about it he left his hand there.

"I thought," said Xavier, when the typing was done, "I thought that we would have our lunch up at Puig d'en Calbo. We will walk up by the chapel and Aspullabalitris will bring the basket up by the road in his cart."

If the girl — it was difficult to think of her as a married woman — had not been there Alain would have protested: it was a long way to the Puig d'en Calbo, a very long way and a steep and dusty way. But he weakly agreed, with the proviso that he must be allowed time to fulfill his promise to visit Aunt Margot, and after a few haphazard remarks they parted, Xavier to the kitchen and Alain to his room for his shoes.

"So that is how it is," he said, sitting on the edge of his bed, holding a shoe in his hand. "So that is how it is."

"Or is it?" putting on his second shoe and standing up.

"Good morning, Alain," she said, kissing him on both cheeks; then "Dear me, you look very poorly, Alain; are you quite well? I could make you a tisane in no time at all. I am sure a nice tisane would do you good."

"No, no, I am quite well, thank you very much. I did not get any sleep last night, that's all."

"Oh, Alain, I hope you did not go to those dreadful creatures in Port-Vendres?" Once, long ago, Alain's youthful curiosity had taken him to the bawdyhouse there, and he had been seen coming out by his Uncle Gaston, Aunt Margot's late husband.

"No," he answered seriously. "Xavier and I sat up in the garden, talking. You know, Aunt Margot, we have no earthly right to interfere; not the least right in the world."

"Come and sit down, and tell me all about it. I am longing to know what he said."

"Well, I am afraid I cannot tell you all that: in the first place it would take hours and hours, and in the second it was not talk that one could decently pass on."

"I see. But come into the morning room anyway, and I will make us a pot of coffee. You would like some coffee, wouldn't you, Alain?"

She had led the way into the quiet, sunny room; she had made the coffee herself, and now the empty cups were cold on the little table.

". . . so you see, I cannot range myself on

the family's side against him," said Alain. "I told you, did I not, that I should probably turn out a disappointing ally?"

"Oh, do not say that; you are not disappointing at all. But how he must have suffered, poor fellow: he must have suffered dreadfully."

"I am afraid he must."

"He should have gone to Father Aurillac. I wonder why he did not go to Father Aurillac." She reflected for some minutes and then said, "Alain, you will probably think me an unfeeling old woman, but don't you think, as a friend, you ought to advise him to take a blue pill and keep to a low diet? Then some mineral waters like Evian or Boulou for the liver?"

"Oh," said Alain, a little staggered, "that is a very dampening view of it." He turned it over in his mind, and said, "But it is wonderful what a pill will do, I must admit. Wonderful and disheartening, the link between one's liver and one's mind."

"Why disheartening?"

"Because one likes to think of oneself as a free agent."

"I am sure, Alain, that all the oil in the cooking down here, and the heavy red wine, is what makes the people so violent, miserable, and irreligious. Have you never noticed that churchgoing and white wine or cider and cooking in butter go together?"

"Well, if he ever consults me, I will tell him what you say. But seriously, Aunt Margot, that is not all that is wrong with Xavier. I wish I were better at conveying the feeling of a conversation: if I had managed to convey even a tenth of the profound sincerity — the shocking . . ." His voice died away.

"No. I am sure that that is not all that is wrong. Oh, I would not suggest that for a moment; though I have no doubt that it has more to do with it than some people might imagine."

"Aunt Margot, if you had heard Xavier last night, as I heard him, you would not speak lightly about it."

"Oh Alain, how can you be so unkind? I was *not* speaking lightly: I just said that — but I will not say any more about it, if it angers you."

There was a short silence, and she said, "But seriously, and very seriously, Alain, I am deeply sorry for Xavier, very deeply sorry for him indeed. I understand something of what he is suffering from, I think. I knew his father and his grandfather." She hesitated, patted Alain on the knee, and said, "I do not include you, my dear, when I

171

say that the Roiges are a hard, unaffectionate family; but they are, indeed, and sometimes, living among them, I wonder whether I have grown like them. I do not say that they have not all kinds of virtues: but they are not an affectionate family. Xavier's grandfather was my father-in-law, of course, and I knew him very well: he was a tyrant. Your Uncle Gaston went in fear of him to the end of his life. He was a very able man, no one could deny it, but he had a wicked, wicked temper, and everyone in the family knew it. Gaston used to tell me stories about their life as children — so hard and bullying and domineering: no love in the house at all, it seemed. You know how much brutal authority a peasant has over his family. It must have been very much like that, only the little peasant children escape quite soon: here in Saint-Féliu with old Monsieur Roig mayor and deputy there was nowhere for them to escape, and he held on to them all to the end of his days. He used to badger his eldest son worst, and I remember dreadful scenes even when Hercule was a gray-haired man.

"And then I saw the whole thing repeated again with Hercule and Xavier. There seemed to be no tenderness in Hercule, none at all. He was quite unloving, at least as far as his son was concerned: but he would not leave him alone, whatever the boy did. It is a dreadful thing to say, but I think it was as good a day for Xavier when his father died as it had been for Hercule when *his* father died.

"And then it was the same with Dédé. Xavier was easily the most intelligent of the three, you could see that very early; but he has made a worse mess of his son than either his father or his grandfather did. He had the poorest of material to work upon, it is true: but it was pitiable to see the poor, wretched little boy . . . Oh it is miserable to think of it, Alain, generation after generation of unhappiness. Old M. Roig was an unhappy, discontented old man, and Hercule, except when he was in court or at some political meeting, was sour, bitter, harsh, and overbearing: I do not think that either of *them* knew why they were miserable, but Xavier is more intelligent. Yet he has no more sense than to think it can be cured by marrying this girl.

"Poor Xavier. Poor fellow. I am sure that that is what it means in the Bible when it says 'suffering for the sins of your fathers.' And I am sure that you must be loving, not only to save your soul, but to avoid entailing misery on the generations — how many generations?"

They sat quietly together, each thinking a

great way off. Alain had in his mind the accusation against his family: it was true, he reflected, they were an unaffectionate lot. They hung together, they were fiercely clannish; they were loyal; but they were unaffectionate. There was very little tenderness in their lives: they admired efficiency and success: but they were unaffectionate. Côme and Renée, Aunt Ursule and Uncle Gaudérique after all these years, Aunt Marinette, Yvonne and her children: there was that peasant hardness remaining, running through the generations. The word "unaffectionate" haunted him, and he wondered how much it applied to himself. He had a fair number of friends, but did he really care whether he saw any of them again? And his family? With Xavier, for example, was his feeling of concern and disquiet caused by affection? No: probably it was not. There was, even now, something repellent about Xavier: or if repellent were too strong a word, at least something that prevented the closeness of friendship.

There was Aunt Margot, of course: he was certainly very fond of her; and Martin in Hanoi. But the others . . .

"These sort of marriages never work," said Aunt Margot, suddenly.

"Why not?"

"Haven't you always seen that they never work?"

"I cannot say that I have. I do not remember ever having seen one."

"Of course, you see very little of life, living there at the back of beyond. Sometimes, Alain — you must not be cross — it is almost like talking to a girl straight from the convent. You have been shut away there among your black men, and you have the same romantic ideas and ignorance of the world. But you have seen a European marry a native, have you not?"

"Yes."

"Then I have no doubt the same thing happens. A few weeks of bliss, then the native family starts presuming, the other Europeans' unkindness begins to be felt, and eventually there are coffee-colored children, neither one thing nor another, and everybody is miserable."

"Oh but come, Aunt Margot, there is no parallel at all. You talk as if we were Bourbons or Hapsburgs or something very grand. But you know that we are only middling bourgeois: in fact this is the first generation to suspect that the word bourgeois is perhaps something less than a compliment. The Fajals are not perceptibly different from us in any way, and . . ."

"Oh, you are not going to start your piece on democracy again, are you, Alain? Of course, I know one has to say all kinds of fine things in public, but no one really believes it, do they? Except the lower classes. They are very good people, often, astonishingly good when you consider what kind of lives they lead, but it is just hypocritical nonsense to pretend that they are not brutish, insensitive, gross, and terribly, terribly limited. There is just as much difference between a man of an educated family that has had money for two or three generations and a laborer as there is between a white man and one of your Hottentots, as anyone knows who has lived or worked among them."

"Is Madeleine a Hottentot?"

"No. But her relations are: and staying here, Xavier would of necessity marry them all. Then think of this, Alain: whatever he may say Xavier values his position very much. A man of his intelligence does not slave away day and night to build up something without valuing it. It will crumble away. You must see that it will. And then he will blame the girl."

"Well, if that is all your objection —"

"But it is not, Alain. If it were, it would just be a dreadful mésalliance and that

176

would be all, but the point is that Xavier does not really want to marry her at all, not *marry* her. He must know that it is madness, at the back of his mind. It is perfectly natural for any middle-aged man to want a very good-looking young woman, and if he is a good man he can easily make himself believe that it is not the young woman he wants at all, but some much grander kind of thing. With Xavier it is this plan of marriage and affection: with my own dear Gaston it was what he called escape from the stifling fetters (or was it mattress?) of provincial life; and with a man I knew long ago — such an attractive man — it was the necessity of a wider, deeper, more poetic experience of life. Then there was the poor archdeacon, you remember, who had worked it all out as a kind of mystical duty   part of a great scheme of love and forgiveness. They had to hurry him away to a monastery."

Alain was already standing up. "You must forgive me, my dear aunt," he said, "but I have an appointment with Xavier in three minutes, and you know what he is like if one is late."

"You will have to run, Alain. Where is your hat? You did not come without a hat? You are dreadfully imprudent, Alain. You should have two or three wives to look after you, like a Monsoon. Here, take this one. It was Gaston's. You *must* protect your head from the sun."

The road was long, of course: it always had been long, but never had it been quite so long, so excessively, unnecessarily long. Their way was the path that led out from the town along the dried-up river-bed; sometimes it was the river-bed itself, rough with loose and shifting stones, paved with old tins and cardboard boxes, and sometimes it was a narrow path by the side.

Why did people bring buckets here, buckets with no bottoms? And while kittens certainly had to be destroyed, who in Saint-Féliu was so eccentric as to bring their corpses up the river-bed a quarter of a mile from the town? It was not a solitary eccentric, either: there must be at least three. The single espadrille. France was littered with single espadrilles, shoes, boots, sandals; occasionally you would find pairs. But in either case they were always a great way from the nearest village or farm, and always they evoked the image of a man hobbling back from some strangely inaccessible point, partially or wholly barefoot. Yet one never met these people. Umbrellas; broken glass; something from which Alain quickly averted his eyes; an iron bedstead; a hat. Some curs from the village, reveling.

This is a fine walk, he thought, looking resentfully at Xavier's straight back; a fine walk, with the putrid dust rising in clouds from their feet.

Xavier was saying how incomprehensible people were: they had a regular collection of rubbish; there were laws to forbid them encumbering the earth with their ordures; yet still they came far out of the town and threw their dirt abroad: it was inconsiderate, undesirable, and above all grossly unhygienic. He delivered these remarks over his shoulder to Alain, and Alain, though he agreed with them all, could not but feel suddenly and strongly on the side of individual liberty, the right of behaving like a mandrill if one chose. He said, in a dogmatic and authoritative voice, that the sun was a better disinfector than anything known to man, and that the danger from this kind of thing was much exaggerated.

He trod on the edge of an iron barrel-hoop; it shot up and struck him on the shin. The blow was exquisitely painful, but that was the least: he whipped up his torn trouser-leg, thinking with hurried alarm of the rusty metal edge and the couch of filth where it had lain. One might have supposed the direct and timely intervention of a minor god. But although the cloth was torn the skin was not: it had been a warning, not a punishment.

Xavier had not noticed at first that Alain was no longer with him, but now he stopped and stood waiting.

"You should look where you are going," he said, as Alain came up. "Did you hurt yourself?"

"No."

"You are limping."

"No I am not."

Xavier raised his eyebrows, and they went on in silence. The road mounted from the river-bed: it was now a broad path running along the edge of an olive grove, and now the last of the rubbish was left behind. Alain began to feel ashamed of his ill-temper and he tried to think of something conciliating to say. They were walking along the best part of the valley now: on their left hand were the olives, an ancient grove on a light fawn ground of withered grass and naked earth, black, rent, and knotted trunks under a cloud of green and silver; and on their right the stream, running low, unseen but audible among the deep green. On either side the walls of the valley ran up in long tiers, one after another, without a single break of scrub or uncultivated land: it was all a dark green now — no earth to be seen between the vines — except that near at hand the gold and red and purple of the grapes showed clear between the leaves.

As the valley ran away from the town, straight inland toward the higher hills, it grew narrower, its sides steeper, and there, in the farther half where the vineyards were terraced one above another in high, short steps, there were many holdings that had never been replanted after the great plague of the 1860's, and they lay like different colored cloths on the side of the hill, always rectangular; some had been replanted with olives or cork oaks, but for the most part the cork oaks were confined to the upper valley, and these lower woods had an intrusive air. Then, in the upper part of the valley again, the part toward which they were walking, there were a few runs of the hillside that never had been planted — too stony, too much hidden from the sun — and there among the thyme and the asphodel stood the tall and lovely pines. Surely among all that, and the mountains beyond, he could find something to say? All that ancient, labored earth, terraced and piled up, turned and turned again since Grecian days. Yet how obstinately a natural remark evaded him. Ordinarily he would have been content to walk along in silence if he had nothing to say, perfectly content, but this was a special case.

"Why is it, do you suppose, that fields and vineyards are always rectangular?" he said at last. "All over the world they are square; never round, not even triangular or hexagonal. It is as if men, even the most primitive, had a natural love for the right angle and the straight line. Yet coins, on the other hand, are all round."

They had just turned off the main path when Alain uttered this remark: they had turned off right-handed up the steep and rocky Cami d'en Jourda, a path some three feet wide, worn deep into the soft rock of the hillside, a path of immense antiquity that led over the crest to the high vineyard they were to visit. It was a scrambling, irregular path; they had to walk in single file again, and the failure of Alain's overture passed almost unnoticed.

Toiling up behind Xavier (Xavier had said no more than the word "Convenience"), Alain said to himself "Well, the onus is on you now. I have done my duty," and he thought in a vague and desultory manner about rectangular fields until they reached the top.

★ ★ ★

The last part of the hill had been a cruel grind, he reflected, as he sat with his back to a tree. He had come to feel the most acute dislike for the springing, eagerly proceeding back of the man in front of him; a dislike mingled with surly admiration. However, that was over now, and so was the long colloquy with Aspullabalitris: so was the enormous picnic. The carcass of the chicken alone remained, flecked with a crumb or two of aspic; one green leaf showed where the salad had been, and two empty bottles lay on their sides by the leaf. They had finished all the cheese and they had eaten the peaches: now they sat in the shade, silent and motionless, while the heat of the day shimmered over the hillside.

They were on their own property now: as they sat there with their backs to the wood, looking out over the sea, the land which ran down from their feet to the town was speckled all over with their vineyards. The cork oak grove behind and the broad expanse of trim, newly reclaimed vineyard immediately below were Alain's. Then came a stretch of garrigue that belonged to Aunt Margot: at the moment it carried nothing but a crop of oleasters, prickly scrub-oak, false lavender, and Spanish broom, but soon they would start clearing the terraces again, and next year or the year after it would look as clean as Alain's; the lines of the half-obliterated terraces would show hard and clear on the hill again, horizontal contours to accentuate its curve and swell, and on the clean, shaley earth there would be the precise rows of young vines, as neat and formal as embroidery. Beyond that, on the other side of the long and winding road, there were the rich old vineyards that had come into the family when Côme married Renée Py, and then to the right of them there was Xavier's land of the Puig d'en Calbo. There the vines ended in the olive trees of the Sorède d'en Calbo, family property again — a share of it was Alain's — and from the end of the long grove it was only a jump to the flat, indifferent vineyards of La Vail, which belonged to Aunt Marinette: and that in its turn did not end before the wall of the town itself. If a man chose to scramble and go a long way round he could reach Saint-Féliu without stepping off land that belonged to a Roig. And that was not all; there were other vineyards away from these, little parcels of land that had come into the market from time to time during the last seventy or eighty years.

Alain's gaze stayed on the town for a moment, the pink, tight mass, all roofs from this height, and then back to the Puig d'en Calbo, a rising knob of ground, a little hill, but lower than where they were sitting, and seen from above it had something of the look of an aerial photograph.

"What are you planting down there, Xavier?" he asked, cocking his eye on a square of brown among the blue-green of the vines.

"Maccabeu," replied Xavier, after a pause. "Maccabeu and a few rows of Grenache."

Alain digested this in silence, and then he said, "I like that palm tree, just to the right, on the Fajals' land. It was always fun to vendange there. I suppose we shall go there this year?"

"Yes, of course. Why should we not?"

There was a small blue figure down by the palm tree: it was almost certainly Jean Pounaou, Madeleine's father. Alain made no comment, but in a little while he passed Xavier a cigar. When they were alight, and the blue smoke was drifting through the trees, he said, "As we were coming up the side I was thinking about fields and land in general, and my conscience began to trouble me about the amount of property we own here. It seemed to me that land, above everything, belongs morally to the man who works on it. Aspullabalitris, for example: he and his people have worked the big vineyard and the two over the other side these fifty years and more: yet we own the land and they do not — never will, however long they go on working it. He knows every stock in each of them, no doubt: I cannot even tell for certain where the Cami Real land stops or where it begins. It looked very bad to me as we came up, I assure you, and I was not at all pleased with the idea of meeting Aspullabalitris' eye. But that was before lunch. It is truly wonderful how the face of the world changes with lunch. Now, well fed — very well fed — and at rest in the shade, I can look upon my agitation as the naive sentimentalities of a beginner in politics: and now, smoking my cigar, I can approve of myself, not merely as a capitalist landowner but as Aspullabalitris' benefactor."

"Yes. Yes, no doubt," said Xavier, who had been paying no attention. "Alain, I want to revert to our last night's talk, if you do not find it too . . ."

Alain made a consenting murmur and Xavier continued, "I am not at all happy, in the first place, about the picture I have given of myself — I begin with the less important point, you see. I do not want to gain your sympathy under false pretenses, and it is possible that I have represented myself as being in a worse state than I am. For example, I do not know whether I made it clear that these last years of biting awareness do not represent my life for all the time between Georgette's death and now: perhaps I should have stressed the fact that I had long periods of dull resignation — between finishing with Dédé and the outbreak of war, for instance, and in the Oflag — and of absorption in my everyday affairs. And if I have given an impression of complete emotional paralysis, it is exaggerated: I always did retain as strong an aesthetic sense as I ever had — not that it was ever very strong: I have never pretended to taste, nor to musical raptures — and a kind of sentimentality, I hardly know how to define it —" (It is wonderful, thought Alain, how he can lay himself open like this and still in some way appear to retain the upper hand.) — "a feeling of poignancy, or rather *for* poignancy. A feeling for the poignancy of a situation, I mean, rather than any pity for the people themselves in it. But I am probably being overscrupulous and refining the point when there is no need: and in all events, this picture of my mind, accurate or inaccurate, is not really very important, because it is a picture of something that no longer exists —

no longer exists, thank God. It was a picture that I was trying to make clear to you so that you should really be able to understand what is going on now, and why I am behaving in a manner that the family considers — how does it consider my conduct, Alain?"

"Demented."

"Very well; demented. Yes, I can hear them cackling. First in hushed voices, almost whispering, 'Mad, demented, *demented,*' then getting louder as one tries to talk the other down, and then in the end everybody shouting together, 'Demented, demented.' But I tell you this, Alain: a man in my condition who does not take the chance that is offered him, the unheard-of, unexpectable chance of escape, *is* demented, demented beyond anything that our dear family could imagine. Put it like this: you must love your God and your neighbor; if you do not, you are damned. And you *are* damned. The not-loving is itself damnation. Now that I have a ladder out of hell, am I going to put it aside because of a few trivial worldly considerations? Considerations, I may add, that I can see as well as anybody else, and which the family, I have no doubt, magnifies out of all proportion."

Alain felt Xavier looking at him during

the pause that followed and he turned aside, pretending to bury the ash of his cigar: the mention of God, hell, and damnation embarrassed him in the light of noonday.

"You know, Xavier, as I said, it is a state of mind that is unfamiliar to me," he said, endeavoring to keep the tone of withdrawal out of his voice.

"Yes, I know, I know. But you can see the validity of it for another mind, can you not?" cried Xavier, eagerly.

"Perhaps I can, to some extent: but my understanding is theoretical. It cannot be anything more, my religious experience being —" He finished with a gesture.

"And yet even without religious experience, even supposing that one were entirely skeptical, don't you see the reality of the present damnation? Quite apart from the question of eternity, the survival of an uninhabited body is . . ." He did not complete his sentence: there was a silence, and when Xavier spoke again his voice was more matter-of-fact; the nervous excitement and tension had gone out of it. "However," he said, "I wanted to tell you about Madeleine. All the rest is no more than a preface to it."

Another silence followed, a long silence, and as the minutes stretched out one after another it seemed to Alain that Xavier had brought himself to a standstill, was unable to begin again.

"I wish you would tell me how it started," he said. "I find it very difficult to imagine."

"Yes," replied Xavier, hesitating; Alain darted a hurried glance at his cousin, and there indeed on his hard and graying face was a trace of the flush that matched the hesitation. "Yes," said Xavier, "I will begin at the beginning." But he lapsed into silence again, and when at last he did speak it was not to begin at the beginning but to wish that Alain had had more time to form an opinion of Madeleine.

"I am less concerned with her beauty — that is instantly apparent, don't you agree? — than with her character, which is something that requires very much longer for its appreciation."

"I am very willing to believe anything pleasant about such a lovely creature. But tell me, Xavier, just how false is the family's account? You are assuming that I know the truth, whereas in point of fact I can only surmise it."

"I cannot tell you how false their account is, because I do not know what they have fabricated: but I can tell you this, if there is anything in it that reflects discredit on Madeleine it is false."

"Well: the briefest summary of what I have heard is this — I will put it as brutally and offensively as possible — your secretary is your mistress, and she has gained sufficient power over you to induce you to promise marriage."

"Yes, I had supposed that that would be the story," said Xavier in an even voice, but there was a dark redness mounting in his face; it suffused his forehead, and he said "Swine, swine," with his throat choked with anger. "Swine," he said, tearing blindly at the ground on each side of him; "Swine."

Alain made no remark, and presently Xavier said, "It is a lie, of course. Madeleine is not my mistress: I am not her lover in the sense this kind of people use the word. As for the marriage they are so frightened of, yes, a hundred times over: I intend to ask her to marry me as soon as the divorce is complete."

"Oh."

"Does that surprise you?" asked Xavier, sharply.

"Not at all," replied Alain; and then he said "I know very little about divorces: is it true that they are very lengthy and complicated affairs? One hears that, you know."

"They can be: they can drag on for years

and end in a stalemate. But in this case everything is quite straightforward — a simple desertion with adultery and certified avowal — and really there is nothing to prevent it from going through as quickly as possible. When these simple cases are delayed you will usually find that it is either a lack of diligence on the part of the lawyer or hunger for additional fees: occasionally there may be obstructive tactics on the other side, but that is less common. No; none of these will apply in this case, I assure you: the first hearing is already over; now there comes the attempt at reconciliation, then after a due interval the decree. The only thing that can cause any delay at all is our uncertainty of the fellow's address."

"The husband's?"

"Yes, the husband's," said Xavier, with a peculiar look. "There has to be a serious attempt at notifying him for the court's attempt at reconciliation. However, that is a trifle. If it were a thousand times graver the divorce would still go through."

"I suppose a lawyer with your standing and political influence could get away with murder."

"If he chose, if he had no reference to futurity, I dare say he could," said Xavier, with a thin smile. "For my part, I certainly could, with murder. It is an unfortunate state of affairs, but it is true. But do not misunderstand me, Alain: 'getting away with it' as you call it is one thing: falsifying the course of a suit of this nature is another. I do not think I could do it, even if I chose: and I certainly have not the slightest intention of trying. No: I can do no more than facilitate its passage through the courts and see that it is adequately pleaded: but that much I can do, and I am doing it with rather more energy, believe me, than any other lawyer in the country.

"But I was going to tell you how it began. It is one of the few cases of this kind where one can find a really satisfactory beginning. She was in my office, typing: I heard the machine stop, and after a little while I went in to see what was the matter — they were papers that I needed urgently. I found her drying her tears with a piece of blotting paper — the tears that had fallen on the documents, I mean. Her face was quite spoilt with crying. I pretended not to have noticed anything, picked up some piece of paper or other, and got out of the room as quickly as possible. When I was back in my own room I found that I was very strongly moved indeed: ordinarily, of course, I should have found the whole thing an irritating, embarrassing scene. I have always loathed women in tears and inefficiency in work. But this time it was quite different, and as I sat there I remembered the many papers I had had through my hands recently with little roundness on them, blisters in the paper: they must all have been tears too. I wondered what I should do for some time: in the end I did nothing, and that is the most significant thing about this episode. I cannot tell you how surprised I was at my own reaction."

Now Xavier had stopped again: it seemed that his eloquence of the night — that torrent of words — had left him, and now as he sat silent there, apparently lost in recollection, Alain began to feel that if the pause went on much longer he would go to sleep. The long, very tiring night was telling on him now, and more than that, he had just eaten a large meal; he was warm through and through without being too hot, he was sitting on a cushion of soft grass with thyme growing through it, and through the shade of the trees above his head bees in myriads passed on their road to the long double row of hives on the mountain-side: his head was heavy on his shoulders and his eyes stung and watered; it was a relief, but a dangerous relief, to close them. He was sitting with his

194

back against a tree; it was not perfectly comfortable, but just to the side of the tree was his jacket, and he had but to slide down on one elbow and fold the coat for a pillow to have the most comfortable bed in the world, sloping, cushioned, scented; very, very inviting. But it would not do, he knew it would not do at all; and to sustain himself he proposed to smoke for a while.

"No," cried Xavier, interrupting him as he felt for his case, "have one of mine: I am always smoking yours." He proffered a long, thin, black cigar, saying "There is more bite in these. I like my tobacco to taste of something."

"This is not what we were smoking last night," said Alain, looking at it dubiously.

"No. These are what I call my specials. I keep them for hard days — assizes and so on. I never give them away."

Alain took off the band, and with a sudden grin exclaimed, "They're Spanish!"

"What of it?"

"Do you mean to say that you smuggle them, Xavier?"

"I do not mean to say anything," replied Xavier, with the contained primness that Alain recognized as his notion of humor, "but it would not astonish me to learn that they were uncustomed goods."

"She was always about the place as a young girl," said Xavier, as if he were carrying on a thread of discourse, "when she was more or less Aunt Margot's companion. She came to practice on the typewriter, and I took very little notice of her, except to disapprove in an unemphatic way: I thought it injudicious of Aunt Margot."

Later he had come to appreciate her usefulness, but it was not until the divorce that she had taken on the proportions of a human being. As her lawyer he had talked with her a good deal, and he had been very much struck by the contrast between her and her family; the family interminably loquacious, raucous, bitterly vindictive, crammed with rhetoric; Madeleine quiet, restrained, wishing only to be finished with the whole business.

"One of the hardest things about being a lawyer in a case of this kind," he said, "is that it is very nearly impossible to interview your client alone. There is not one of the family who does not feel like a principal in the affair, and you find your office stuffed with father, mother, aunts, cousins, everybody, and each one is determined to present his or her view of the case. They justify themselves and they pour hatred on the other side as if you were the judge, as if they gained something by winning you over to their side. They always reach your house in an overexcited condition, and very soon their company manners and respect give way and they are all shouting away together, striking attitudes, red in the face and sweating, vociferating: it is very tedious and very difficult to manage. It is also nearly impossible to get a clear and truthful answer to the essential questions: the family always knows better than the man or woman concerned, always interrupts, and always, always, they either lie or distort the answer to improve the appearance of their case. You can never convince their idiot cunning that it is useless, worse than useless, to deceive their own lawyer. There is nothing that gives you a lower opinion of humanity than a divorce case, unless perhaps it is a disputed succession: in either some of the bile and venom spills over on to the lawyer. However experienced and hardened you may be, you feel dirty after one of these scenes."

Generally, he said, the injured party enjoys the scene as much as anyone — more than most, indeed, being the center of attraction, dressed for the part in a kind of mourning and supported and cosseted by one or more toad-eaters. But here it was different: the one desire and aim of Madeleine was to dispatch the business in hand, be shut of it; she loathed the whole proceeding, and sometimes she was short with her family. They, for their part, bitterly resented her reserve: they were nearly as angry with her as with Francisco. They could not understand that she had not come to them long ago when she had first known that Francisco was deceiving her; they felt that they had been wrongfully deprived, and in their indignation they filled the interview with as many hard words about her willfulness, headstrong ingratitude, and self-sufficiency as Francisco's crime.

Xavier had a certain talent for mimicry, and he reproduced part of one of the early interviews.

XAVIER: Did you ever see any letters that he received from women?

MADELEINE: No.

DOMINIQUE: How can you say so? There were dozens of them, I'm sure.

THERESE: She tries to keep things back, Monsieur Xavier: I know very well that she has seen them. I'll swear to it in any court: I don't mind what they say.

MIMI: How about that bitch at Paulilles? Do you mean to say she couldn't write? Eh? Of course she did.

JEAN: What bitch at Paulilles?

MIMI: The one he got into trouble, of course. She wrote to him: ask the postman.

JEAN: Oh, the thief. When I get my hands

DOMINIQUE (*weeping*): It's no good. If she won't confide in her own mother she won't confide in Monsieur Xavier. It's always been the same.

JEAN: on him

THERESE: For shame, Madeleine, for shame. Why don't you show the letters?

JEAN: he'll get no more girls into trouble.

MIMI: I'd give her such a shake if she were my daughter.

THERESE: Don't you know your duty to your parents? Of course you must have seen some letters when you have been going through his things, the traitor.

JEAN: The bandit.

MADELEINE: I never did go through his things.

DOMINIQUE: It's no good talking. It's always the same. She *would* marry the good-for-nothing. For all we could say she would have him. I went down on my bended knees . . .

XAVIER: Now —

THERESE: Oh but it's true, Monsieur Xavier; she never would come and confide in her mother or her aunts.

JEAN: The pederast.

MIMI: Listen to me, Madeleine. You answer Monsieur Xavier properly and tell him what letters you have seen or I will . . .

XAVIER: Quiet, quiet, quiet.

JEAN: Quiet, can't you? Let Monsieur Xavier . . .

ALL THE WOMEN: Be quiet, Madeleine, and answer Monsieur Xavier properly.

In the end he was obliged to forbid the family, and rather than have set interviews he obtained the remaining facts by scribbling her a note and attaching it to her work: she would type her response and so it would pass without words.

"I have never known another case where I could do that," he said, "because in general it is essential to interrogate your witness, to have a personal interview with him, to be able to estimate the amount of falsehood in the reply. You must not be suddenly let down in court by your own witness, who has successfully deceived you, but who is penetrated by the other side. But with her I knew that what she replied was true; and that is a very unusual certitude, believe me, and a very agreeable one.

"But in spite of my shutting the family out, I am afraid she still had — still has — but a sad time of it with them. They want to know every detail of what I have said, what she has replied (and they tell her what she should have replied), and what the exact state of progress the case is in. They never believe what she tells them: they are always certain that she is keeping something back, and they harangue her about openness, a mother's rights, and so on. It is the women mostly, but Pou-naou does his share when he is at home.

"Yet these are not bad people at all: I should emphasize this point. I know that Dominique has kept many families going by giving them credit through hard times — giving it decently, with no grudging or unkindness. Old Jeanne, for example, Espourteille's widow, has not paid the shop a sou in three years, although she is no relation at all. They are kindly, reasonably honest, hard-working and loyal and they are very well liked in their quarter; but they are utterly at sea with a woman like Madeleine. They have no conception of how her mind works. They have not a single scrap of self-discipline or restraint in their natures, and they regard a person who suffers quietly with indignation and resentment.

"They have calmed down a little now, but at first they were beyond all bounds. For example, they went to that dismal house where

Madeleine lives and destroyed every vestige of painting or drawing that the fellow had left behind him, and when Mimi — that is the strong-minded one — found that Madeleine had put some of his work in a cupboard, she gave the poor, miserable, suffering girl a blow that knocked her flat.

"I think that those women between them would have picked and badgered her to madness if they had had her to themselves; they never left her alone for an instant, and all the time they were harrying her to come and live with her mother: she wanted to have a place of her own where she could at least be sure of peace at night. She held out for a long time, but they are untiring, that sort of women, and I dare say they would have worn her down: in the end I told Pou-naou that they would have to stop it, and he told them, effectively enough, to leave her alone at least to the extent of living where she chose."

In spite of his efforts to keep awake, torpor had been creeping over Alain: he held his cigar near the ash, so that the advancing heat would spur him every few moments, but still his eyes would glaze and his mouth would open and the voice at his side would become an even, soporific, united sound, not words at all but a kind of drone;

then he would blink, and the blink would prolong itself and his head would sway forward until he was brought up with a jerk by the imminent loss of balance or by the fiery sting of his cigar. But these last words of Xavier's pierced his dulled ears and brought him suddenly to life.

"You said that to Pou-naou?" he exclaimed.

"Said what?" asked Xavier with a frown; he was five sentences farther on, and Alain had interrupted him.

"Told him to make them leave Madeleine alone and let her stay by herself in her house."

"Yes. Does that strike you as odd?"

"Very, for a lawyer."

"I think it was fairly evident to Pou-naou by this time that a special relationship existed."

"Oh: I see. I had my chronology wrong. I had supposed — but it's of no consequence."

At what period, then, had this occurred? It would be so much easier to have it all tabulated. His tired brain could not cope with the arrangement of events now. And after all he had the main facts, the main facts.

Now Xavier was talking about her loneliness: how sweet the opportunity for unkindness had been to many in the village; the ugly, spotted girls and their loud whisperings and runnings to see; the laughter behind her. Yes, he could understand that.

". . . case of this kind. It is very strange to see that in some way the virtuous women feel themselves offended. The deserted woman is despised, not because she has failed to retain her man . . .
wounded animal hated by the others . . .
the strong element of possession: they seemed to feel that now that she was no longer owned by Francisco she reverted to them . . .
status of widows in India . . .
and for ever they said 'I told you so' . . .
the only pleasant aspect, and that a very small one . . ."

The cigar was out now. It had been out for some time, and Alain's chin was sagging down nearer and nearer to his chest. The words were seeping through to him now like the sunlight through the leaves, separate splashes of gold in the great dark shade that grew and grew.
"was old Camairerrou . . .
sit with her . . .
would bring her fish . . .
Aunt Margot, too, at first; and there I must admit
mistaken . . .

though in general could not advise the association
but natural good breeding . . .
and innate good sense . . .
expressed in beauty."

Alain's breath was coming deep; he could hear it, and though the words which passed on the surface now were alive with interest for him, he could not forego the luxury of his closed eyelids, and slowly, slowly, with a sense of wrongdoing, he let it drop, let it drop, and let his light go out.

Chapter Six

"You have been here a long time now, Alain," said Aunt Marinette, with heavy meaning in her voice.

"Yes; yes, indeed," replied Alain, thinking quickly for some remark that might divert her. "It seems as if I had been home for ever. The vendanges will soon be here. I am looking forward to that. It is true, isn't it, that they have already started in the plain?"

"We had all hoped that this dreadful business would be over before the vendanges," said his aunt.

"Yet still it persists," said Uncle Joseph. "Still it persists. I ask myself, why does it still persist?"

"Be quiet, Joseph. And we begin to wonder whether you are not on Xavier's side."

"You have been encouraging him, Alain," said Uncle Thomas, accusingly.

"He is afraid of Xavier," said Côme.

"Perhaps you *want* Xavier to marry this woman?" asked Renée.

Alain glanced toward Aunt Margot, but she was aloof, a neutral, and she would not catch his eye.

"No," he said to the family in general, "I disapprove of Xavier's plan. I disapprove of it entirely, and I have told him so."

"Then why are you still staying there?"

"If he has not given in and come to his senses, why are you still staying there?"

"You ought to make your disapproval publicly known, and make a common front with the rest of the family."

"I am staying there for a good many reasons," said Alain. "One of them is that I want to see more of Xavier and of Madeleine . . ."

"You've seen plenty of her, haw haw haw," said Côme.

"Be quiet, Côme," said Renée.

"What influence I may have is . . ."

"I wish I'd seen half as much, haw haw haw," said dirty Côme.

Uncle Joseph began again, "I ask myself, why does it still persist?" And in a tone of preternatural cunning he answered, "It is because of the iron vehicles that the Germans brought in nineteen forty-two, and the iron mines on the coast." His voice rose, "But when the garden god his weapon waves . . ." They led him away, and in the confusion Alain slipped out of the room, out of the house altogether. For a moment he was inclined to disregard his Aunt Margot's voice behind him, to feign not to hear it — and indeed it was but a weak and bleating sound as the old lady hurried after him.

"There," she said, panting as she took his arm. "How fast you walk, Alain; I had to run. What a basket of crabs they are."

"You might have said something," said Alain crossly.

"My dear, what is the use? The only thing to do with this sort of people is to tell them clearly what to think before they get over-excited, repeat it once or twice, and then be silent. It is of no use to attempt an explanation. Besides, I had no idea at all of what you meant. When I went to stay with Eulalie you were breathing fire on behalf of Xavier: now you say that you disapprove of his plan. How was I to know whether you meant that or whether it was just for the benefit of the family?"

"Oh, it was true enough. How was Eulalie?"

"Quite well, I thank you. But you must not try to put me off, Alain. So you told him that you disapproved?"

"Yes."

"But you are still staying with Xavier?"

"Yes, of course I am. Why not? We did not start knocking one another about, you know, or throwing knives. Women always tend to take a very melodramatic view of a disagreement between men: in just the same way they are always very forward in urging them to go off to a war. No: we are on perfectly civil terms; and I have no doubt we shall remain on them."

"Alain, that is not a respectful way to speak to your aunt."

"No, it is not. I beg pardon. It has been a trying morning."

"You must remember, my dear, that I am very much older than you. When you were an ugly little fat boy in a black pinafore I was already a middle-aged woman."

They had reached Aunt Margot's house. "Come in for a little while," she said. "We will sit on the bench under the vine, and you can tell me everything that has happened."

Passing from the hard, brilliant glare of the white sun into the shade of the trellised vine was wonderfully agreeable: they sat not so much in a green shadow as in a soft, diffused green light, a positive light that sprang from the leaves themselves. The air was fresher, more breathable by far, and Alain, sitting on the smooth, worn marble, looked up at the great hanging bunches and felt his temper improve.

"Now have you got everything you want?" asked his aunt. "Have you got something to smoke, and have you got something to light it with?"

Alain patted his pockets. "No," he said, "I smoked my last cigarette at Aunt Marinette's."

"I thought as much. Then we will send Thérèsine for a pack: I have no intention of sitting down for a long gossip with a man who is fidgety and cross for want of tobacco."

Old Thérèsine had bobbed and taken the money: "I will go to Mimi l'Empereur," she had said, fixing Alain with her beady eye, and nodding her head with emphasis.

"Jean-Paul's is nearer," said Alain, staring along the path where she had gone. "It is nearer by quite five minutes."

"That is where she will go, no doubt. She only said it to see what you would answer. She is an impudent old woman, and I shall be obliged to turn her off one day."

Alain was not sure what to make of this. Was he being stupid, he wondered, or was it really not worth while being so tortuous?

"If you will stretch for that bunch over

your head, my dear," she said, "you will be able to reach it without getting up."

They sat for a while in silence, sharing the grapes, and then she said, "Did you enjoy the concert, Alain?"

"The concert? Oh yes: it was not bad at all. It was all very passionate, and there were lots of drums. They played bits of *Scheherazade* and *Prince Igor* and Liszt's noisiest piece. I enjoyed it very much. I like that kind of music."

"You used not to. It used to be Bach or nothing for you, or Bach and English madrigals."

"Yes. I was a very cultured young man, was I not?"

"You were a very solemn young man for a time. But do you really like that kind of music now, Alain?"

"Yes, I do. I like having my emotions thumped now and then. I have a record of Ravel's *Bolero* in Prabang that I have nearly worn through. But one does not have to dislike the one to like the other, surely? They seem to me different things; or addressed to different parts of one's body, at any rate."

"Still, I should have thought that all that banging and leaping about would have appealed only to a more . . . What did Xavier and Madeleine think of it?"

"Xavier was not able to come (as you know very well)," said Alain, turning to her with an ingenuous expression, "but Madeleine enjoyed it very much. It was the first concert she had been to."

"So you pointed out all the instruments?"

"Yes, I pointed out all the instruments."

"How kind you are, Alain."

Thérèsine brought the cigarettes, and Alain, who had been expecting her with some impatience, lit a cigarette at once. He wondered how Aunt Margot would come round to the aquarium, which he had also visited. Ah, the luxury of a cigarette when one has waited for it, not too long, but longer than one wished. He drew deeply on the tight, frail tube, and it gave, subsided a little between his fingers and thumb as he forced the air in through the glowing end. The saltpeter spat and crackled, the little core of heat warmed the inside of his palm, and he swept all the smoke down into his lungs.

"She will certainly come round to it," he thought, as he let the smoke out in a long sigh, "but how?"

But she disarmed him by saying "Your father had exactly that way of breathing in and blowing out like a dragon." It took her some time to reach the aquarium: it took her half the length of the cigarette; but with a turn to the sea, the fish in it, and a transitional inquiry about the state of the car, she reached it.

"Yes," he replied, "the aquarium was looking very well. There were sea horses." He paused. "It will surprise you to learn that Madeleine was there too. Xavier was coming, but he was detained again, so I drove her over."

"Indeed?"

"Yes. And I was seen with her on the afternoon of the twenty-fifth as well; and I walked with her from the corner of the rue Pasteur as far as the wall on the evening of the twenty-seventh. I was alone with her from half-past nine on Wednesday . . ."

"That is not at all witty, Alain. Or at least if it is it does not appeal to my sense of humor. It is very clever and modern, no doubt . . ."

"No, my dear aunt," said Alain, laughing, "you must not mind me. It is only that I cannot help wondering very much how it is that Côme can flaunt about all over the department in his car every week end with a different wench without anybody taking any notice, whereas if I am once seen talking to a young woman it is commented upon, reported, discussed; and if I walk five yards with her unaccompanied, well —"

"I do not know what you are talking about, Alain," she said, "and I think we had better change the subject."

She is still cross, reflected Alain: she never could bear being laughed at. However, I will make a handsome amend. And after a pause he said, "I think it will please you to know that I have come round to your way of thinking."

She looked at him with the keenest interest, but she said nothing, and he continued, "As I was saying to the family this morning, I disapprove of Xavier's idea, and I told him so."

"I am so glad," she said, quite thawed. "Do tell me what you said. Poor Xavier."

"Yes, poor Xavier: that is true enough, my God. But nobody ever seems to have thought poor Madeleine . . ." He broke off, for Thérèsine was coming down the path again.

"It is Mme. d'Oultrera," said the old maidservant. "She says the blue Virgin has got the moth."

"Oh dear, oh dear," cried Aunt Margot. "Show her into the drawing room, Thérèsine. No, I left a bottle of brandy there. Beg her to step into the morning room, Thérèsine, and hurry, hurry. I shall have to go upstairs. Alain, my dear, do not move. Sit there in the cool with your nice cigarette and I will . . ." She hastened away.

"Tell me what you said." Yes, that was what he intended to do: but it would be difficult, very difficult, to summarize, condense, report in the first person, and still convey something of the original. Not that it was particularly complex in this case, but there was always this difficulty of communication: the near-impossibility of conveying any but the most definite concepts, even to an attentive and sympathetic mind. Two and two make four; that, yes: but "I told him that I thought his conduct improper and he replied that he did not agree" — what did that convey? Or "It is a bronze of rather more than life-size, a nude lying on her back." Or "It is a picture of mountains in rain and cloud: they are very steep and ragged and pine trees grow on their sides." Or "The coda consists of a piu mosso version of the first subject, commencing pianissimo and working up to fortissimo."

No: what one needed was a new method of communication altogether. For this kind of thing a film with a sound track would answer very well: he ran it through his mind.

SCENE: *The first terrace of Xavier's garden. Xavier and Alain are sitting in long wicker chairs, drinking Banyuls and eating little Spanish cakes. Enter from the left Dirty Côme and Renée: they are obviously ill at ease and they advance, mincing and scratching themselves, the whole length of the terrace. The first greetings are made. A silence.*

RENEE: We have come to talk to you very seriously, Xavier.

COME: That's right.

XAVIER: Listen to me, Côme, my friend: listen carefully.

(*A silence.*)

COME: What to?

XAVIER: Just listen; that is all. If you do that you will not provoke me. You do not wish to provoke me, do you, Côme?

COME (*looking apprehensively at his wife*): No.

RENEE: We chose today, Xavier, because we happened to hear that that woman was away.

XAVIER (*aside, but audibly to Alain and probably to the others*): Sour yellow beast. (*To Renée*) Your informant was mistaken. If you will wait a minute . . . (*He rises.*)

RENEE (*disconcerted but flouncing*): Oh indeed. No, don't trouble yourself, Xavier. I

216

think we had better go now. Côme. Good-by, Alain.

(*Exeunt*)

XAVIER: That got rid of them quick enough.

ALAIN: Poor Côme was in a muck sweat.

XAVIER: Poor devils. It is enough to make you wish each of them a dose of rat poison out of charity, seeing them together.

ALAIN: You are in a very good humor today, Xavier.

XAVIER: Yes. This divorce is getting along very well; faster than I had expected. It is nearly at the top of the list.

ALAIN: That is all you are waiting for, is it?

XAVIER: That is the essential. I must say that in my experience I have rarely seen such a simple, straightforward case — nothing to go wrong, no hidden snags, nothing to prevent a clear and immediate decision. Yet I am afraid of it: I know that nothing can go wrong, but I invent flaws in the legal presentation of the case and worry about them until I have got the papers again to reassure myself. I was on tenterhooks all through the formal attempt at reconciliation — I imagined a hundred ghastly accidents. But of course he was not even represented.

(*A pause.*)

ALAIN: I cannot help feeling — you will not mind my saying so — that you have a somewhat one-sided view of marriage. Or rather, of this marriage.

XAVIER: One-sided? I do not think I understand you.

ALAIN: By one-sided I mean selfish.

XAVIER: Selfish? Upon my word, Alain . . . I propose giving the material advantages of a marriage that any family in the whole province would welcome gladly, any family, the d'Oultreras or anyone. I say nothing of the care with which I would surround her, nor the affection. Consider the material side alone — you do not have to have half your experience of the world to appreciate the importance of it. Think of the position I can give. That sounds conceited, even a little absurd: but if you take it in relation to Saint-Féliu it is less so. Think of what I can do for her family. No, I intend to give all I can — give with both hands, and give spiritually as well as materially. That is not very selfish, I think?

ALAIN: That is not really what I was thinking of. Though in passing I may say that the position you would have to give would be very much less considerable after such a marriage than before it.

XAVIER: What a familiar sound that has.

ALAIN: I dare say it has. And I will say this, too, Xavier, that I *do* speak from interested motives, at least to some extent, and I do speak with something of the family's voice. I am not joking in the least when I say that all the Roig blood in me curdles, and rightly, when I hear you talking of giving with both hands — giving more than you have a right to give. I mean it in sober earnest, Xavier, when I say that you have a greater duty to the family than you realize. I say this to clear my conscience; for I know you hardly believe it.

XAVIER: You are right: I do not think you are fundamentally interested in money or property.

ALAIN (*shrugging*): Well — When I say one-sided I mean that you seem to take Madeleine's inclination and consent very much for granted, and her subsequent happiness. Have you reflected enough, I wonder, on the fact that you are at least middle-aged, and that neither you nor I could be called a beauty?

XAVIER: I do not take her inclination or consent for granted at all, Alain: believe me, they have caused me more thought and trepidation than ever they cause half your romantic lovers. But even if I had done so, I still think that her subsequent happiness would be secure. I am middle-aged, I agree. But that is not without its advantages: for one thing, I am no longer afraid of clichés, and I can say, and believe, that this is the sort of marriage in which love will come afterward. I do not pretend that she is passionately in love with me: of course she is not, and it would be very unsuitable if she were. But I think I may say, without being too fatuously complacent, that she has a sincere friendship for me, a real liking; and that is the best foundation for a marriage.

ALAIN: It is not very romantic.

XAVIER: So much the better. She had enough of romance with that young swine Cortade. As you say, I am no beauty: well, he was, and what did it amount to? People who live together no longer see one another after a year or two. I think that all this talk of good looks is very much overdone, and I am sure that most of the current notions about romantic love are so much twaddle, piffle, flim-flam. You know as well as I do that 'romance' is a recent invention, a leisured invention, and that it hardly touched the lower classes at all until the coming of the cinema and these appalling magazines, 'books,' for the semi-literate. Our fathers and grandfathers married out of prudence and good sense: it answered admirably well. And even now, you know how and why nearly all peasants marry. No, no; the tinselly nonsense has hardly any relation to what is really felt: mutual interest and subsequent good-liking are infinitely more important. I tell you, Alain, I am deeply convinced that one grain of genuine affection is worth all your poetry and Saturday-evening raptures. Furthermore, I will say this: for ninety-nine people out of a hundred it hardly matters at all whom they marry. Providing the man has a reasonably pleasant character and an adequate income, one is as good as another. You make the mistake, I think, that so many sentimental people make: you attribute too much personality to individuals, much too much importance to those few little traits that make one man superficially different from the next. Perhaps it is a natural reaction from your impersonal, objective work.

However, that is entirely beside the point, as I must obviously except myself from what I believe to be the general rule. Yet it would hold for practically every marriage I have ever seen.

ALAIN: I dare say you are right. But we are not discussing a female philosopher, are we? If the world in general supposes that it is starving for what it calls romance, it will be very unhappy if it cannot get it, whether it exists for the majority or not. It is asking rather much of a young woman to see these matters through the eyes of a middle-aged lawyer.

XAVIER: She has a most uncommon amount of strong good sense: and one does not always have to count experience in years.

ALAIN: There is still a considerable difference in age.

XAVIER: How you do harp on it, Alain. Though upon my word I cannot see any vast discrepancy: I never have been able to. After all, think of Jean Marty. Théophile Fabre. Abdon Ostalrich. Françoise Delmas married a man older than her father. They are all perfectly happy marriages.

(*A pause.*)

ALAIN: Old Fifine used to terrify me when I was a little boy by telling me that I should be put to the new tower.

XAVIER: Well?

ALAIN: It was a new tower that she said was going to be started very soon.

XAVIER: Well?

ALAIN: You know the story of the towers?

XAVIER: I know it as well as you do. And let me tell you, Alain, that I very much object to being parabled at: it presupposes a gulf between the understanding of the teller of the parable and that of the hearer, and in this case the supposition is as unjustified as it is offensive.

ALAIN: I had not thought I was being so obvious. But there is a reason for parables that you may have overlooked: they are a refuge for those who wish to say something disagreeable but who lack the right or the moral courage to do it. I was going to remind you of the hideous legend (if it is a legend) of a child having been built in alive to insure the firm standing of each of the original towers of the wall. I would then have mentioned the tales of bell-casting: a maiden thrown into the liquid metal so that the bell should have a clear cry. Then I should have said that I felt very deeply indeed that a strong tower or a well-toned bell had no right to existence on those terms.

XAVIER: Well?

ALAIN: And if I had said it with all the convincing power that profound sincerity is supposed to give, you might have agreed that a parable has another advantage, that of being more moving than a direct harangue.

XAVIER: Well?

ALAIN: That is all.

(*A long silence.*)

XAVIER: A parable can have its uses, no doubt: but for our purposes it is too indefinite. Your meaning, for example, is by no means clear.

ALAIN: Tell me, Xavier, in all this do you suppose that your first motive is to give happiness, or do you suppose that it is to possess an object on which to exercise and develop your power of affection?

XAVIER: Where is the distinction?

ALAIN: Put it like this: is it your intention to marry her willy-nilly, and make her happy whether she likes it or not? If you do, if you mean to use your force of character and position, her present situation and her family's pressure, to oblige her to marry you from obedience and weariness, so that you will be able to begin your experiment —

XAVIER: It is not an experiment. If only you had understood me thoroughly you would see that there is nothing experimental about it.

ALAIN: I insist that it is an experiment. It is not a previously worked out chemical operation, nor an arithmetical sum; of course it is uncertain, and of course it is an experiment. You are trying to buy a human being as your guinea pig, and paying for it with influence and position: it is a thing you have no right to do to a human being. You have no right to do it, and if possible even less right than none, because the experiment is certain to fail. No: let me have my say. I repeat, certain to fail. Do not think I am unsympathetic, Xavier, I am not that. I cannot tell you how moved I was when — how very much I feel for your shocking predicament. But I am absolutely certain that this is the wrong solution. You have mistaken yourself. You are undergoing a flare-up of your sexual appetite and you want the physical possession of a young and very beautiful woman: you will not admit it consciously, and you have rationalized it into this more acceptable form. There is nothing in the world easier than being deceived by one's body. I do not say that your state is not a dreadful one: what I say is that this is the wrong solution. I will propose one, though you will neither believe me nor consider it. You should go to that miserable, wretched building the other side of Port-Vendres and come away with one of their abandoned children. A little girl orphan, not a boy. You could give it a home; you could give it everything, and upon my honor I would not say a word if you were to leave it every last sou you possess and every scrap of land. You could give it everything: and if in a matter of days you did not start to love it, I know nothing whatever of human nature.

XAVIER (*coldly*): You are very eloquent,

my friend, but all that you say is based on the assumption that I am wholly repulsive to Madeleine. If you are mistaken in that, do you not see that your entire rhetorical structure collapses? Or am I to take it that you are better informed upon the subject of her feelings than I am?

ALAIN: No. I am only more objective, that is all.

XAVIER: Then I am to understand that you have no authority for your remarks other than your own unaided powers of observation?

ALAIN: Xavier, if you are going to adopt that high and mighty legal tone we might as well talk about something else. I never did like it and I will not stand it now. You are not cross-examining a hostile witness.

XAVIER: Am I not?

CURTAIN

". . . so I suggested that he should adopt an orphan and bring it up."

"And what did he reply to that?"

"He did not make any direct reply. He suddenly appeared to be seized with the idea that I had been commissioned to tell him that Madeleine could not bear the idea — perhaps *by* Madeleine. Or perhaps it was that he thought that I was taking altogether too much interest in her. I don't know. But the conversation came to a stop, and I was very glad that I was engaged to dine with the Gaudériques that evening; the atmosphere was uncomfortable, to say the least."

"So Xavier is jealous. Dear me, that makes everything much worse."

"I suppose he is: I would have thought he had more sense. It was unfortunate that I had promised to run Madeleine into Perpignan in the car the next morning."

"Of course, she is a very, very attractive creature."

"Isn't she, though?"

"Alain, it would be dreadful if in trying to rescue Xavier from this trap you were to fall into it yourself."

"Dear aunt. Dear aunt. Sometimes I wonder . . . I talk to you on occasion for an hour or more on end, believing that you follow me at each stage, and then at the end I find that I might have been talking Cambodian. You can still speak of my trying to rescue Xavier from a trap . . . Really, Aunt Margot, I thought you had more penetration."

"It comes to much the same thing in the end, does it not? Do not be cross, Alain."

"I am not cross. Only sometimes I despair."

"So Xavier is quite wrong in being jealous?"

"Of course he is. I wish I could make it clear that it is as absurd for him to think of being jealous of me as it is for you to talk about Madeleine trying to *entrap* him, or to *entrap* anybody else."

"You quite bewilder me, Alain, talking so vehemently. Be a little calmer, if you please. We are not a political meeting."

"What I wish to make abundantly clear is the fact that what I said to Xavier represents my true feelings on the matter: it was not a series of diplomatic lies designed to detach him from a designing hussy, nor to rescue him from a *trap,* as you put it. The only thing that was not completely true was my toning down of Madeleine's aversion and my omission of a good deal more that I could and should have said. I should have said that after a great deal of thought I had come to the conclusion that the marriage would be disastrous, not only because it would not answer Xavier's expectations, but — what is more important — because it would be complete and utter misery for the girl."

"But what is it that makes you so angry about it?"

"You would be angry too, Aunt Margot, if

you saw that poor girl . . . She does not give a damn for Xavier's position or money or anything else. All she wants is to be left alone. She respects him very much, I believe; he is kind to her, and she is touchingly grateful. But it makes her shudder when he touches her, and he is always touching her. The idea of a physical relationship must be unspeakably distasteful: and yet that is what Xavier and the others will bring her to if it goes on as it does at present. Can't you imagine her family pushing her? Those stupid, greedy aunts of hers? Nag, nag, nag, nag, nag, with all the indomitable persistence of stupid women. They never leave her alone for a second. They would never for a moment allow her to leave Xavier's employment — oh it is sickening. She would much rather work in a salting house, or sweep streets for that matter."

"Why doesn't she?"

"She feels that duty and gratitude have some call on her."

"What a lot you have learned about her, Alain."

"It is obvious enough, if you live in the same house." He fidgeted with his matchbox, abstractedly taking a match out and putting it back again. He said, "People are terribly hard to one another. It quite hurt

229

me to hear you say 'trap.' There is something so hard and grasping, commercial, about the idea. With your knowledge of Madeleine, I wonder that you could have said it."

"Well, perhaps I should not have said 'trap.' I am sorry that I did. But, my dear boy, are you quite sure that you always know when I am speaking seriously?"

Alain considered for a moment, and then smiled at her. She continued, "And are you sure, quite sure, about your own feelings? Altruism is so rare, don't you think?"

"Oh, I make no claim to altruism. I should be very happy, from the family point of view, to see Xavier restored to a commonplace lawyer, and if that can be combined with preventing a thoroughly amiable young woman from being condemned to a repulsive marriage, I shall be quite satisfied."

"Well, I hope you may be right. If it were anybody else, I should doubt it."

"You can be quite easy. I will give you the clearest proof in the world of it. Quite easy. My solution is simple: it is to effect a reconciliation between Madeleine and her husband. If you are right in saying that she is eating her heart out for him there should be no difficulty on her side, and as far as I have been able to gather his difficulties were

230

mostly to do with her family, lack of money, and lack of congenial employment. I imagine that his infidelities have no particular significance; I hope not, at any rate, for my intention is to offer him a settlement in Banyuls or Collioure, a certain amount of encouragement, and a certain amount of money. As for a house, I am sure we can find something among the family: without going any further I can think of the house over the far end of Côme's cellars in Banyuls — it has been empty for years. Then as for encouragement, you could do a great deal for him with Church patronage, could you not? Certainly enough to set him on his feet."

"Yes, I suppose I could. There is the chapel at Costaseque . . . Yes, I think I could, if he would paint sensibly."

"Then as for money. There is nothing like ready money. What do you think the family would put up?"

"They would expect you to do it all, if you suggested it."

"I dare say they would. But I have no intention of doing so. You would have to propose it to them. If it were just a simple question of buying a woman off they would come running with their contributions, I am sure: but this is a little more complicated, and it needs somebody with your authority to make them understand. What do you think of the idea?"

"I think it is a splendid idea. But, my dear boy, you had no right to say those unkind things to me about 'grasping' and 'mercenary.' You are quite as bad as I am, if not worse. For example, I should never have thought of using the painting of the new Madonna at Costaseque as a means of keeping the family property intact."

"Oh but come, Aunt, you *know* that that was not what I meant."

"No, of course it was not, my dear. But first you have to find the young man."

"Yes: that may be difficult. I cannot very well discuss it with Xavier. I have great hopes of Marcel, however, and I do not think he will fail me."

"If you obtain anything from Marcel you will be cleverer than Xavier. Xavier worried him every day for a fortnight with no result."

"So I understand. Still, I have great hopes of him."

Chapter Seven

Marcel Dumesnil was the family's one contact with the arts. He was a writer, and he had married Louise, Marinette's Louise. The family regarded him with mixed feelings, for although they could not be proud of their connection with him as a person, yet there was the fact that he was a writer, and that, in a country where even the most depraved of literary hacks is regarded with some degree of respect, that weighed enough with them for them to be able to say, not without complacence, "Louise and her husband Marcel, Marcel Dumesnil, you know, the writer."

Xavier and Aunt Margot had never been able to stand him for a moment, but the others were sufficiently resigned to the marriage to be quite civil to him, and in this instance Alain sided with the rest of the family: he could never feel strongly enough about Louise to dislike Marcel (in a few more years Louise would have grown still more desperate and would have done still worse for herself) and indeed although he had seen very little of him — they lived in a house behind Collioure, in the hills, far from Saint-Féliu — he even had a kind of sympathy for him. The feeling did not amount to liking or to fellowship: it was difficult to define, but it was real enough to evoke a kindness in Dumesnil, who more than once told his wife that Alain was the only one of her family he would pull out of a quicksand, in the happy event of their all being plunged in it up to their necks. It was real enough, too, for Alain to have kept silent when he could have exposed Dumesnil to the brutal mockery of the family, the despised bourgeoisie. It was a curious story: Dumesnil had begun writing early and his first work, the usual autobiographical novel, had enjoyed a surprising success. It had not sold a great many copies, but coming out at a time of unparalleled dearth it had been well reviewed and it had even been awarded a literary prize, a reputable literary prize. At first this had astonished the young Dumesnil, but soon his changing estimate of his own worth, catching up with his success and overpassing it, made all this appear normal, and he wrote his second novel with a light heart and a running pen. It was little more than a rearrangement of the first, and as the first had been almost entirely derivative this imitation of an imitation made his publishers shake their heads for a long time in anxious doubt: however, they accepted the manuscript and printed it. "This is easy," thought Dumesnil, hurrying on with his third book. He was quite sure that he had found the formula for writing novels, and when he sent off this third manuscript he waited for the friendly, enthusiastic letter of acceptance with a sense of agreeable anticipation: no doubt, no qualms.

The rejection, the prompt and unequivocal rejection, was a horrible shock. He was married by this time; he was set in his delicious role of the Literary Wonder and already he had gone too far along the road of superiority, too far in his expressed contempt for the bourgeoisie to retreat: nothing could sustain him in his dangerous attitude but continuing success. But the second shock, the truly disintegrating shock that came but one post later was a copy of the reader's report that a friend in the publisher's office had procured for him: this report and the office memoranda pinned to it showed him a naked opinion, unglozed by the least civility. "This MS is really too amateurish . . . There is nothing left of the unconscious freshness, the appealing naivety which was the only merit of the first book and the only reason for tolerating its tedious, bumptious, adolescent cleverness: this quality, such as it was, had almost entirely vanished in the second novel, and now there is not the least trace of it. This piece of work is even worse than the last — wholesale plagiarism. M. Hertzog was mistaken when he thought that there was a possibility of the development of a mature talent . . . the public is very gullible, but not to the extent of swallowing this . . . cut our losses." And the final damning note scribbled by the head of the firm, "Nothing more to do with this man."

It was a terrible blow, all the worse because with the unsubmerged part of his mind he agreed with the criticism. Yet he had been so sure. He had been quite certain that they were deceived. When he had seen these men he had played the part so well, he thought — the impulsive, sincere young writer. But they had watched him behind their politeness: they had not been deceived, and perhaps they had laughed at him afterward.

He did not succumb at first. He went through the manuscript: worked hard upon it. Naivety had impressed them. He spent hours and hours in his room, putting in naivety and charm. But now he was uncertain, all adrift: was this intellectual or was it just dirty? Could you be naive and still say sodomy? He could not tell any longer, and when the new typescript was ready he looked at it with haggard desperation.

No one would publish it. He tried again, sending it out under an assumed name, hoping to pass as a beginner once more, a new young man with possibilities: but it was no good.

Still his efforts did not cease: he began a new book, and he worked as he had never worked in his life. Freshness, originality, and ingenuous clarity were his aims; but now all was tentative, doubtful, unsatisfactory, and as the book progressed it went slower and slower. He was afraid of finishing it, and it dragged slowly to a standstill.

But in the meanwhile there was the continual necessity of keeping up his position, of defending himself, and with a shock he realized that the good opinion of his plain and stupid wife was vital to him, as vital as her inherited competence; he had thought he despised her. As he had never fundamentally believed in his own talent he had naturally despised those who did look up to him, and yet as he possessed a sour and lively vanity he despised those who did not. Or more exactly, although he felt himself to be a genuinely superior man, he believed that his superiority lay in a general intellectuality rather than in any one particular talent: his writing was a "front," a weapon against the profane. It was not necessary for him to believe in the "front" so long as he could believe in what it was intended to guarantee. The writing could be bogus, admitted to be bogus, so long as the overman was there. And so to move from this shifting ground of half-deception to outright falsehood was easy for him: he was hardly conscious of any change.

At one time he had been employed in a printing house, a firm that handled pornographic books, the pamphlets and "literature" of cranks and charlatans, the catalogues of accessory shops: he paid them to set up a title page with his name on it and this he had bound with the body of a Swedish novel. He presented the result as a translation of his own work. This was a great success, in some ways greater than the triumph of producing a new book of his own which anybody could read; and he found to his surprise that it gave him nearly as much satisfaction. It was the reaction of Louise that interested him most, that was most important to him. Perhaps she had not known of the decline in her devotion: perhaps she did not consciously redouble those innumerable ministering attentions that buoyed him up: but Marcel was vividly aware of the difference. Once again it was the finger on the lips and the whisper "Marcel is working," the shielding and the cosseting, "Marcel must not be upset," the willing submission to his vagaries: above all, the religious subjection of her mind to his.

Six months later he repeated the experiment, this time using the body of an English book: it seemed to him particularly suitable because like his own novel it had the names of streets in Paris scattered up and down its pages. Like so many writers he was a man of little or no formal education and he did not think there was any danger in all this. He knew no foreign language himself; he had a quicker intelligence than those around him; and it followed that he did not believe that anyone else could really read English or Swedish. They might for examinations; but not in real life.

Then it was verse. This was a little harder to explain, but the fact was that he did not choose to publish verse in France at present, and while translation was evidently not the same thing still it was something, and they importuned him so . . . And of course one has to think of America. It was harder to explain, but it was worth the risk, for poetry covers all idleness, all lack of present success, all dependence, all rudeness, all eccentricity: poetry need never wash or shave, may lie with its neighbor's wife, drink gin, haunt foreigners: poetry is already clothed in immortality; poetry prophesies, speaks holy; may abuse God.

But unknown to Marcel then, the stranger Alain, far away, had worked with English colleagues and with Indians: he had attended conferences on tropical medicine in India, England, and America, and he had read papers to the learned societies there; he used the language almost daily in his work. And so when he stood in front of the bookshelves in the Dumesnils' house, looking by express invitation at Marcel's works, he opened the pages to find a language nearly as familiar as his own.

Dumesnil's choice had been wretchedly inept: it was a book that had run into hundreds of editions, and it was as well that Alain's back was turned to the room, for in the first moment of recognizing the novel (he had read it in Singapore and again on a never-ending train that took him to Lahore) he was unable to govern his countenance.

He flapped back the title page to make sure that he was not mistaken; then he glanced furtively into the French volume with the same name and compared the opening phrases. He was conscious of fat, commonplace Louise behind him, flushed and almost pretty in the expectation of his praise, and of her husband, preening in the background, a prickly, surly, difficult fellow, but pathetic in his insecurity. Pathetic, at all events, to Alain, who did not have to see much of him.

It was not in fact a very difficult situation to carry off: all he had to do was to take no notice and to say the usual polite words. It was, as one might say, a negative duty, but in his own estimation he accomplished it rather well: he gave a certain amount of pleasure where he could have spread certain misery, and when he went away he felt inclined to be pleased with the object of his benevolence.

In spite of a strong temptation to tell Aunt Margot (it would so have delighted her) he had said nothing to anyone, and now, these years later, as he went on his difficult errand, his errand of drawing information from Marcel, he could not refrain from glowing with smug self-satisfaction at his former restraint. If he had indulged himself then, he would be without a single weapon now: but as it was, he could approach the house behind the pine trees with all the happy confidence of a blackmailer with irrefutable proof in his pocket.

Marcel saw him coming up the long, winding path and instantly thrust the novel that he was reading under a pile of papers on his desk. He took up the attitude of a man thinking and bowed himself over a sheet of virgin paper. From the corner of his eye he could see Alain appearing, vanishing, reappearing among the trunks of the umbrella pines; then there was the sound of the door and Louise's loud, harsh voice — the loudness of surprise and the emphasis of welcome. Then her voice dropped suddenly, and as she tiptoed creaking through the hall with Alain Marcel could hear her whisper and in his mind's eye see her significant gesture toward the study. He heard the furtive closing of the drawing-room door, and when he had waited five minutes or so he got up and went into the hall. He called Louise, and when she came he said, "Oh, there you are: do you know where my old red notebook is? I have looked for it everywhere."

She said, "It is on the top bookshelf, I think. Alain has just come."

To her, privately, he made a martyred

face, but aloud he said, "Oh, I am so glad. I had just finished my work." He pushed past her and went into the drawing room: Alain came forward from his place by the bookshelves and shook him warmly by the hand. "I was just looking for the English translation of your book," he said.

"I do not keep it there any longer," said Marcel. "I was afraid it had a little air of ostentation, you know?"

Louise left them after a little while: she was due to go to Saint-Féliu, as Alain knew very well.

"Am I not Machiavellian?" said Alain to himself, with a feeling of excitement as if he were playing a dangerous game, but playing it well and with a reserve of strength unknown to his adversary.

He had been talking for some time about Marcel's books, always harping on the English translation: Marcel seemed pleased on the whole, but he was reticent when the translation was mentioned; he tried, not without skill, to lead the conversation in other directions. Now, during a pause, he was beginning to think that Alain was not as agreeable as he had supposed, and that perhaps he would get rid of him on the plea of an urgent article.

Alain, equally silent, was wondering

whether this was not the moment for a direct attack; he wondered, too, whether Marcel had not already seized his drift — whether perhaps (with a sudden inner chill) he had not some prepared defense. He looked thoughtfully at him: Marcel looked very self-contained, somewhat withdrawn, sure of himself, detached: it was disturbing. But this detachment arose from a cause that Alain could not suspect. Marcel was devoted to his own person: he could not think himself handsome — the looking-glass denied it twenty times a day — but still he was devoted to it, and this devotion extended even to his own smell. Often, when he appeared to be listening, to be listening with a certain abstraction of mind, meditative, critical, and aloof, he would be taking secret gusts of himself, bowed over his own bosom; and he would draw a more real satisfaction from this than from many an acknowledged sensual delight. How could Alain divine that this was the base of the silence that weighed heavily now in the cool and darkened room? He could not, and the silence grew heavier and to him more formidable. He was beginning to feel unpleasantly nervous, and abruptly he pushed away his chair, took two or three turns up and down the room and came to rest at the open window: his back was to Marcel now, but still his voice, low-pitched and conversational, was perfectly audible in the room.

He stood with his hands on the inside of the windowsill, resting his weight on them like a shopman standing at his counter: his shoulders were hunched, and his shape, dark and colorless, cutting out the light, oppressed Marcel. And Alain, standing there on the edge of his crisis, did not see anything of the stretch of garden in front of him, nor the pine trees falling away to the sea: he did not see the hoopoe that walked on the grass, suspicious and wary because of the voices from the house, but still too pleased with the garden to fly away. Every other moment it would stop, cock its head, half-raise its crest, and crouch to take off; but then it would change its mind and hurry with busy steps about the parched lawn again. But Alain saw nothing of this; and Marcel, when he was alone again, saw as little.

Alone again, moved by some obscure feeling of substitution, he had taken up exactly the same position as Alain: to replace that dark, ominous, expressionless, and dominating back he stood there, swaying on his hands, his shoulders hunched; and like Alain he saw nothing.

Now, hunching there, he made his familiar secret indraught and now he fancied, or was it more than fancy? — that there was a feral smell, the rank smell of terror, the smell of a wild animal that has just escaped from a trap, an animal running free at last, free from great danger, but with the smell of dread strong and harsh upon it still.

In Saint-Féliu they were at her again. The three women and Jean Pou-naou. They had insisted on her coming back for the meal, and she had been too weary to find any good excuse. It had begun before the meal, even while Dominique was cutting up the bread, and now that the plates were pushed away it still went on.

They wanted to know if Xavier had said anything. "He must have said *something*," pursued Thérèse. "He cannot sit there without a word."

"Your mother has a right to know these things, Madeleine," said her Aunt Mimi. And now they would go on again, round and round the same track — openness and confidence, the right to know, the wickedness of secrecy: conjectures, cunning plans. She would tell them if there were anything to tell; but what was there she could say? It was going slowly on and on, but there was nothing fresh each day.

What contact was there left? She would be loving if she could: indeed she loved them very much. They meant to be kind, she knew; but looking round that familiar room she saw it with a stranger's eyes. Her mother's face, poised in the act of speech: it was like a woman she had seen before, but long ago. And yet for all these years she had been so kind; so good and loving, and so kind.

They had switched on to Francisco now.

"They say he was seen in Perpignan."

"Who says?"

"La Patta: he was there."

"She's writing letters to him," said Mimi with a scream.

"I'm not. Truly I'm not," said Madeleine, but Dominique and Thérèse had taken the alarm. They were shrieking. How could she tell them that it was quite dead? They would not listen: they were so frightened and grasping that they could not believe it even if they heard. The voices went on screaming in the little room. Denunciations, threats, recrimination.

"I always said . . ."

The man's voice cut through and said, "If he comes back, I'll serve him out. I'll serve him out, by God. Mother of God, I'll rip him up . . ."

On and on: she had heard it so often. Now Mimi was shaking her by the shoulder. "Say he is a bandit. Say he is a bandit." The force and venom gave her the voice and aspect of an evil woman.

"He is a bandit," said Madeleine.

This was a great victory. They had always tried to make her say that, and now she had: they had gained something, and now they were quieter, almost kind to her.

It had died slowly, but it was dead. The last dying hurt it gave her had been that woman passing through again in her car — that first one, Claire Delahaye. They had passed on the high road, months ago, one second's recognizing glance: then the next day she found that she did not mind.

It was Xavier again, what he would do, what he possessed: everything that he had ever said was passing in review, with commentaries from them all.

If only they did not start on Alain again: they had canvassed his presence fifty times, the concert, the drives to Perpignan, the walk. Was he a valuable ally, drawing his cousin on by jealousy? Was he a danger? What was the wisest trick?

"Oh God, do not let them start on that," she prayed. She could bear the rest, all the sorting out and prying, the picking over of her life: but would they leave just that un-touched, if only for today?

The passage of time. The passage of time: it is a platitude to say that it is not measured by the turning of the hands of a clock. Nor, Alain reflected, by any mechanical means: the engine of the car was turning at three thousand revolutions a minute, a well-nourished steady hum with the feeling of great power in reserve; the wheels turned at — he tried a complex piece of mental arithmetic: his speed was sixty-one kilometers an hour, and the diameter of the wheels . . . But the answer came out to an improbable figure, and he abandoned it. It did not signify. The essence was that the last twenty-seven kilometers had been rendered tedious beyond measure by a huge lorry, a long-distance hauler who would not let him pass. The great blind square tail of the monster was blundering along at sixty-one kilometers an hour with a cloud of dust behind it, and in this cloud Alain had chafed the whole length of the straight and narrow road that led south from Rancy. It was not that he wished to go so very much faster; this was not far from the speed he would have chosen, for he liked a gentle, gliding cruise on an empty road (and it was much too fast for the lorry, which was bumping about on the crown of the road in a way that would have made the forcing of the passage horribly dangerous) — it was not the slowness that made the time so tedious in its passing; it was the constraint.

And yet it was not tediousness that counted in the right measurement of time: far from it. Indeed, almost exactly the reverse was true, for if one came to measure it by some truer standard than the clock, the vast deserts no longer counted; at the time they seemed interminable, those gray years in station waiting rooms, in aeroplanes, in ships, but once they were over they were finished and done with forever, while those apparently shorter spaces spent in intense and significant activity grew and grew, spread themselves . . . yes, the right measurement would be in terms of nervous energy, in units of personal anxiety. Or if not of anxiety, then of tension, nervous expenditure.

Before him there was a wide patch of road, a sudden widening with a border of yellow sand or gravel, very close and quite short. His foot went down on the accelerator and at once the steady, rather languid hum changed to a full-throated roar; a great force thrust at the small of his back, and leaning over the wheel he shot forward: he was embodied in the machine, he was the machine's eyes, gauging the space between the lorry and the yellow verge. Now his foot was on the floor and he was surging furiously past the long gray bulk of the lorry's side. A glimpse of the sullen, angry face of the driver and it was over: he raised his foot gently and blew a hoot of derision on the horn.

Now, with the road open before him he let the speed slacken and the roar of the engine die; the needle sank back to seventy-five and he relaxed in his seat. What a lovely thing that engine was: the car — it was Côme's car — was a vulgar, scarlet affair with exaggerated lines: but the engine, that was something else again. And it was surely very strange that Côme, an earthy soul if ever there was one, should be capable of appreciating it. There was no doubt at all that he did: when Côme spoke of a new sodium-alloy valve, or triple carburetion or any of the mysteries of the car's interior, the habitual knowing leer of the "big operator" left his face, and it was replaced by an open ingenuous look of enthusiasm, an earnest look that made him, in those moments when he held a balanced crankshaft in his hands, almost pleasant to look at. Côme, confronted with religion, patriotism, the arts, the seven virtues, could only respond with a horse-laugh: yet there was the capability for genuine, unselfconscious admiration in him. Why this partial development? Perhaps it was an immense shyness that spread over everything but this one small admitted area. Poor Côme: and decent Côme, on this occasion. He worshiped his rakish, super-charged, scarlet monster; he had the utmost contempt for Alain's driving; yet he had lent it for this journey with hardly more than a whine — and that without knowing why Alain had been obliged to go to Paris with such urgency. It would not, after all, have been decent to borrow Xavier's car. There was another car with a personality: a rigid, square, and upright car, black and shining, a car that ran perfectly well, though in a grudging, irresponsive way, in spite of its twenty years.

But to revert to the question of time: it had struck him very forcibly when he was wandering down the interminable boulevard Saint-Germain that the only significant time is that during which you are aware of being in the present. At that particular moment he was living solely in relation to the future — the future that would start when he found the right number and that would become the living, active present when he found the right door — and at most other times he lived almost entirely in relation to the past, to the present that had gone before. He had time and enough to chew over this reflection, for he had started at the wrong end of the boulevard, the comparatively clean end by the river, and he had the long and weary walk all the way along it, past the poor, railed-in dirty ghost of the abbey, past the tourist cafés with the charabancs outside — those strange places where the Americans play at being French and the French at being American — past all hope of quiet and peace, until he came to a gaunt tall building, high and comfortless, with all the sordid venom of a slum and none of that picturesque vitality a slum may have.

It had been a curious interview. At least one of his preconceived ideas had been scattered in the first moment, for he had had to go down the hard and angular naked staircase instead of up it. It had been naive to suppose that a poor young painter must, from the fitness of things, necessarily live in the garret, a romantic notion, too: but it had disturbed him to go down into the underground passages, the square, dark and humid passages that wandered vaguely in the gloom, like the approaches to a fifth-rate hell. He had been disconcerted, too, when more or less by chance he walked in at Francisco's open door, intending only to ask the way, and found himself in the middle of a roaring scene. A large, fat young woman was addressing a harangue to a man sitting in a wretched attitude on the floor: both stared at him, and Alain, with some words of excuse bumbling in his head, was about to step back into the darkness when the young woman, crying with great bitterness "Oh, I leave him to you," thrust her way out behind him and slammed the door. As she went, Alain noticed that she was far gone in pregnancy.

That was the beginning; ill-omened, awkward, disagreeable. Francisco must have changed a great deal, judging by the descriptions Alain had received in Saint-Féliu: and in fact he had coarsened terribly; all the fineness of his face had sunk under fat, and fat had invaded his body. The wonderful litheness and grace was gone, and now he gave the impression of bulk, muscle-bound bulk. The same black hair (too much of it, and curling down his neck) and the flashing teeth were there, but the hair was dusty, unwashed, and the teeth that had gleamed in a sun-tanned face no longer had the brown for contrast: and the whites of his eyes were yellow. The eyes themselves were shockingly diminished by the fat around them. Yet still he had the leaping spirit of his earlier days. Or had he? Was not this confusion of canvases, this vie de Bohème, these old patched fisherman's trousers all a little too good to be true? Too good to be true, together with the eager, boyish, confidential, would-be infectious enthusiasm? And were not these newspaper cuttings rather too carefully preserved? And then the paintings themselves . . . Primitive, of course. Very well: so primitive. No objection; though perhaps there were rather too many primitives in the present world already. But what was the explanation of the big and glossy book of reproductions on the table? Reproductions of other primitives. And why was the book covered up with a cloth — surreptitiously covered after he had been there a little while, covered while he was looking at a series of drawings?

Would he have been deceived if he had not seen Marcel? For Marcel had supplied Francisco with his attitude, and Marcel had assured Francisco that his one paying line was to remain the simple, wide-eyed fisherman. Marcel had not been sure that his advice had sunk in: he had told Alain, with some vexation, that Francisco had for some time opposed his wishes, had prated about "integrity," had covertly gone on painting in a manner as un-primitive as he could manage; and he feared that once Francisco was away from his immediate influence he might very well continue in this disastrous way. "Disastrous," he had repeated angrily, for he had a real affection for Francisco, and he wished to put him on the right road. Privately, of course, Marcel thought the pursuit of any of the arts ridiculous for a man, allowable only if the pursuit were undertaken with the intent of diddling the art snobs: for Marcel did not believe that any sane man gave a damn for painting, nor for sculpture, music, or poetry, and that those who pretended to were either fools or were trying to make something out of it.

Would he have been deceived if he had not seen Marcel? It was difficult to say, and indeed it was a useless speculation, because having seen Marcel, and having stripped Marcel naked, he could not be deceived by hearing Marcel's words all over again, uttered seriously now from an ingenuous countenance. It was strange to hear them repeated, occasionally distorted but generally exact enough, but with the ludicrous difference of stress: the difference between the violent cynicism of Marcel's voice, aping the phrases that were to pierce the bourgeois hide to the soft marshmallow vulgar heart within, and the solemn, earnest tones of Francisco saying the self-same words. Alain had heard them twice, once as it were an accomplice, the second time as the legitimate audience: the effect was to take a great deal of the humanity away from the second speaker and to give him the strange, disturbing air of an automaton.

And yet what did it all prove? Did it prove anything more than that Francisco had been very much too much influenced in his vocabulary by an older man who was, in his eyes, a considerable writer and a man of great abilities? Could not his painting still be perfectly valid?

Alain looked carefully at the pictures Francisco showed him. He looked very carefully, and as objectively as he was able: apart from the primary necessity of piercing through the painting to the painter, there was the fact that Alain was going to have to buy one of these canvases, and he felt that he might as well have something that he would like. But try as he would, he could not see anything much in them. There was a certain talent, and the color was effective enough sometimes; but there was so much gesticulation, so much emphasis, so much literature. They were not very convincing. It would have been difficult, very difficult for them to have made a convincing show in the circumstances: Alain acknowledged it and made a great allowance for his foreknowledge, his kind of moral eavesdropping, but even so he grew more and more oppressed by his certainty, his ever-increasing certainty, that they were based in affectation, that they were slick, pretentious, and above all that they were dull, dull, dull.

Francisco was pleased with them, however. His voluble explanations and the exertion of bringing them out and putting them on the easel made him sweat: the atmosphere that he created reinforced his self-esteem, and his face shone — shone a little too greasily, in Alain's opinion. But by this time it was clear enough to Alain that he did not like Francisco, and that he never could like him.

And yet again, what did the painting matter? A very good man could be a wretched painter, and certainly a very good painter could be a miserable, vaunting failure as a man. It was absurd (however tempting) to make an equation of moral and artistic worth.

But studied insincerity in painting? It was a kind of forgery to which a man would have to shape his whole life, was it not? In that case the falsity would run clean through: the man would be lost, drowned in his own pose. This was not a case of technical ineptitude, nor of aesthetic insensitivity, nor even of vulgarity of soul: no, although all those entered into it, they were nothing compared with the conscious forgery.

Drowned, gone for ever under his own pose, extinguished, a man would be, after such a course. Or at least, if he were not quite lost, as Marcel for example was not lost, then he would have to have a little secret inner life, where he could live with some truth to himself. But that was not the way Francisco was made, surely?

This much was clear. Francisco was a sentimental; that is to say, he could be as hard as nails when he chose, but when he was confronted with a set "pathetic" situation, he dissolved. When Alain, forcing himself to the task, spoke of Madeleine solitary, nagged, mocked, and deserted, Francisco wept like a woman at a cinema. But it was equally clear that this susceptibility to simplified and dramatic situations had involved him hopelessly: it was clear too that he could not resist gestures, gestures of the grander kind, those that involve leaving all, eternal renunciation, perpetual fidelity. Involved hopelessly. He had already "left all" for the middle-aged cinema actress, and then for the fat young woman: he had eternally renounced a great many people and things, and now he was being perpetually faithful to three women at once and presumably to his art as well.

But would the involvement have remained quite so hopeless if Alain had mentioned the establishment, the money settlement? Alain had plowed on to the end, unwilling to leave anything unsaid that he felt he ought to say — this although he was by now convinced of the inutility of his visit — but he had not mentioned the money. He might have come to it in the end if he had not gradually become aware that Francisco was enjoying all this, that the fellow's vanity was charmed by the idea of broken hearts behind him, and that Francisco was pumping him for details that would flatter his conceit.

Alain had gone on out of a kind of obstinacy, and, it must be said, out of stupidity, for he knew very well that although he went on talking his reason for being in that room, that horrible underground room, lit by the unshaded glare of the daylight lamp, had come to an end, and that all he had to do was to pay for his picture and go away. Yet he had stayed a good half-hour after he knew that it was hopeless, after he knew that he was deeply convinced that this man had no integrity left, that he was selfish to the ultimate degree, that he was shallow, callous, and a fraud, and that his only remaining quality was a kind of flabby charm. He was no longer concerned with the painting, true or false: for him the great fact was that buying this fellow back would be an impossible solution for Madeleine. Better, far better, to abandon her to Xavier.

"The beefy, wicked lout," he exclaimed in anger; and pressing on the accelerator to escape from the thought of the past he made the big car run faster and faster down the white road between the trees.

Chapter Eight

By eleven o'clock the great heat of the day had begun: in the enclosed valley the sun beat down from its height on to the sloping vineyards, tilted to receive its power, and the heat reverberated from the stone walls, the stony paths, and the crumbling, powdery earth that lay naked between the newer vines. Higher up on either slope, beyond the terraced vineyards, the hills were brown, light khaki brown, desiccated and parched beyond description; the bare soil that stood between the crackling, withered scrub blew up in acrid clouds whenever the breeze stirred over it. There had been no rain now for seven weeks, and it was hardly conceivable that in the spring those same higher grounds had been green, a brilliant living green, and that the goatherds had been afraid to let their flocks go up there, for fear of gorging.

From the too-perfect sky, from the scorched and sun-drenched hills behind, and from the arid slopes above, the eye fell with gratitude to the vines: everywhere, on all the unnumbered terraces, there were the vines; and among the vines the vendangeurs, moving among the dark green rows; for now the grapes were ripe, and now the families were assembled, friends, cousins from as far as Marseilles and Toulouse, relations to the farthest point of kin. For them the vendange was a feast, a ritual, a time of strange excitement, more intense by far than the harvest of the corn in the north, more religious.

These hillside vendanges were entirely different from the vendanges in the plains, where the enormous, dull, flat vineyards stretched in precise commercial rectangles to the horizon, and where the pickers, hired troops from the towns and mountain villages, labored under the driving of an overseer: here there was no hired labor, here there were no flat rectangles, for here the vineyards, cut by the loving hands of the generations, climbed in mad shapes up to the limit of fertility, hand-planted in basketfuls of carried earth, hand-grafted, hand-hoed; the evidence of hands, the uninterrupted generations for how many hundred years? They had found the pieces of a jar from Samos when they dug to enlarge the well some twenty years ago. Long enough, at all events, to have changed the face of nature, to have given the whole of the lower mountain the appearance of — Alain, though he straightened for a moment to regard the mountain, could find no term for his description. There was the valley: it was covered with vineyards, with tiny white box-like houses, rose-tiled and prim; it had been labored upon, cut, hewn, blasted, and piled into one vast coherent pattern: it was like nothing else, and there was no point in dragging for a simile.

But the hands that had done this work had been harder hands than his: every year, every single year, those hands like his had been stained purple by the grapes, sticky purple hands, covered with dust; but under the stain and the dust they must have been horny, callused, protected against the use of tools, familiar with the rub and scratch of branches. Already there was one blister on his right forefinger, in the crook of the joint, where his minute sickle pressed for every cut, and there was probably another developing there where his left hand seized the bunches. Certainly there were no less than three gashes on that same left hand: at the beginning of the vendanges he always nicked that blind left hand as it groped darkly in the leaves for the main stem, which his right hand, equally blind, was to cut with the bright-edged sickle. Three certain gashes, if not four: in a spasm of professional dismay he remembered the case of tetanus that he had seen in Prabang — risus sardonicus. "That is the most perfect example of the risus I have ever seen." He remembered the tone of Martin's voice: yet Martin was the most humane of men, and he had struggled for that man's life as though his own depended on it.

Their backs, too; they must have been much more supple. For a long time now his own had been a broken bow, painfully mended with sinews, creaking as it straightened. It was not surprising: since half-past five it had been bending, straightening, bending. For these were not the high-trailed vines of the Georgics: these were bushes, waist-high or lower, and the bunches hung low to the ground. They were bushes that were cut right back to the stump, the black, gnarled, tortured stump, in the winter, and it was only the one year's growth that stood now, shielding the grapes, tangling crisscross in the older rows where the stony soil was rich; dusty and worn outer leaves, a few of them already scarlet.

He was out on a little triangular apron of vineyard by himself: it was a patch of soil, poised over an enormous boulder, and there was no room for the main body of pickers, who were moving along the rows above him. They were laughing and talking still: the handkerchiefs on the women's heads were brilliant in the sun. The Fajals were there, over on his right. Certainly they were there, helping to pick the Roiges' grapes as they had done every year since Roiges and Fajals had begun in Saint-Féliu: they were neighbors, vineyard neighbors, and the Roiges picked the Fajals' vineyard in their turn. Certainly they were there. Aunt Margot did not understand this: but neither did she understand the primordial importance of the vendanges. She did not see that the vendange was a truce of God: or rather she did not know the god whose truce it was; and if Alain had tried to make the explanation clear he would have had a very short answer, with "unhealthy mysticism" and "modern earthy nonsense" in it. Or she would have looked at him with an amused and cynical eye, saying nothing.

They were laughing up there. The effect of breakfast must still be with them, he thought. That immense breakfast eaten down there by the little square white casot: sausage grilled over the embers of a fire made from last year's vine cuttings, hard-boiled eggs and anchovies, sardines, ham, cold chops, black pudding, white pudding, and olives, Roquefort at nine in the morning and welcome, membrillo; bread, bread, bread, and a dozen skins of wine. Perhaps it was the last Hellenic touch that lingered with the Catalans, that feast on the brown earth in the morning.

But nine o'clock was long ago. Longer ago still, removed to another time altogether, was the beginning of the day, that dewy beginning under a sky still green, when the grapes were exquisitely chilled by the night and the dust had not yet begun to fly.

There was no more left on that vine. Half straightening with a grunt, he moved his basket and himself on to the next. This was a muscat; he recognized it with joy: the pale, indented leaves hid great swagging inverted pyramids of grapes. His left hand plunged in and found a tight and solid bunch: as the sickle cut the stem the bunch fell heavy in his palm. He bit a mouthful from it, huge golden grapes, cool still, despite the hours of sun. Kneeling, he devoured the whole cluster of them, and now his throat was clear of dust. There was a refreshment — nothing to equal it. For the last hour he had been picking the small, dark, fiery, thick-skinned Grenache, no good for thirst at all. A wonderful crop, big, firm bunches, a bucketful from a single vine, a deep satisfaction in the taking; but no good for thirst now that the sun was up. The muscat vine; he remembered it from former years. Once he had known where each one was, scattered up and down the vineyard for the relief of the people working there, but now he remembered them only when he reached them.

The little solitary patch was done, and at the same time the party above him reached the end of their row, of their half-dozen parallel rows, and because they worked in a team they stopped for the stragglers. Alain clambered up the slope to join them, emptying his full basket into the waiting tub as he went. There was Madeleine, coming down with her grapes, looking at once quite suitable and madly out of place — suitable, because she was dressed in an old black overall with a spotted handkerchief on her head, and suitable, because she so obviously belonged there, knew exactly what to do, did not feel herself extraordinary; but utterly incongruous as well, for on that day of all days she was in looks, in the bloom of her looks and gilded with the sun; and as she came down, with the broad basket on her head, her hands filled with overflowing grapes, she moved with incredible distinction. Her fine head poised, her dazzling complexion, rising from that old and dusty dull black pinafore would have made an unaccustomed stranger stand and gape: the most romantic view of ancient Greece, seen through the haze of three thousand years, the Golden Age itself, the vases, sculpture, and the verse, promised nothing anywhere like this.

She was in spirits too, that brilliant day: she carried the basket on her head from wantonness, and her face was alight with transient happiness.

"Mare de Deu," said Alain, and to interrupt his stare he began to crush the piled grapes down into the tub with a heavy stone, making room for these fresh baskets full.

They began on the higher rows, working from one stone path across the vineyard to the next: Madeleine had the high row, and Alain coming up last took the top row, the row above hers. He was working faster now; he had to, to keep up with her; and all down on his right there was the steady snip-snip of the women's secateurs and the murmuring of voices. Now the grapes fell into his hand, heavy, dusted with the bloom, bloom on purple, for now they were in the Carignan, grapes big as muscats, dark and perfect: the vines sprang up as the weight was taken from them.

She was holding up an enormous bunch for him to see. "Oh wonderful," he replied, and he was glad to have a reason for his smile.

Below there was a shout of laughter: someone had left a bunch uncut, and they splashed the crushed grapes on his face. It was red, blood red, the juice that trickled down his cheeks.

Along the row. Here the big Carignans had grown so high that when he crouched he was in their shade, green and comfortable; but he was not noticing his unhinged back any more, nor the heat, nor the dust in his shirt, on his face, in his throat. He had three newly grafted vines with nothing on them, and he was well ahead of Madeleine. Stepping across to her row he cut the grapes of her next two vines so that she could catch him up. The small boys ran between the rows, emptying the baskets, bringing empty ones.

"At the end of the row we shall find a muscat vine," he said, and she laughed as though what he said was witty. He had remembered that muscat: it was the old vine where they had buried a toad, to make the thief turn black and swell, if ever he came stealing in their grapes. Alain had gone in the night and released the toad, his heart beating high as if he were the thief under the moon, in the strangeness of the night; but the toad had died.

They were at the muscat stock picking off the very best to eat, throwing the others into their baskets. "Té," she said from the other side, throwing him two the size of little plums. She had never tutoy'ed him before; and when he spoke French to her he had said vous, though no doubt knowing her from a child (if he had but remembered her) he could very well have said tu. Xavier vouvoy'ed her, but so he did to the world in general.

There was a renewed outburst lower down the slope: the little boys were piping; everyone was standing up. "There is no more *room* in the semal," said the middling boy, his voice cracking with indignation. "The semals are full," said the smallest boy. Several people cried "Pau has not taken away the full semals. En Laurens has left the empty ones down there. Pau has not taken the full semals away."

"The semals are full," said Alain.

Madeleine answered "Yes," and they stood looking at the full tubs of grapes ranged at convenient points along the wall.

The middle-sized boy was treading one in a vain attempt to make space for the baskets and pails that were cluttered at its foot.

"En Laurens," shrieked a woman, and some others shouted Pau. But both the men were far away, down behind the casot repairing a broken carrying strap, swearing and bawling instructions to each other so loudly that no distant cry could ever reach them.

"This would never have happened if Monsieur Xavier had been here," said an old woman, a poor and distant cousin, exasperated by the heat and dust. They all knew that dinner would not start preparing until they had reached the top of the piece of Carignan, and suddenly everybody grew cross and discontented.

"Sitting down there. Lying in the shade. For shame, the idle, do-nought, selfish . . ." and they shrieked their names again.

Côme was red with anger. "Why can't they organize things?" he asked. "Why does Xavier have to choose this day to be away?"

"They would not be sitting there playing if Monsieur Xavier was here," said the old woman. "Pau. En Laurens." "Pau," screamed the little boys. "En Laurens Cortals."

"Why don't we ever have a mule?" asked

Côme. "*They* have a mule over there." A mule was indeed threading its way down the steep vineyard next to theirs at that moment, charged with a tub on either side: it was a beautiful mule, with crimson harness thick-studded with brass nails.

"Why do *we* never have a mule?" asked Côme. He turned in exasperation to his neighbor, but this was Jean Pou-naou, who could not very well reply: they were neighbors, not relations, and they could not criticize the absence of the mule. They were to keep silent, though the work was stopped; and silent they were, for that and other causes. Mimi and Thérèse were there, but all day they had been like ghosts, quite dumb, unnatural and constrained.

Alain slid down over the wall: the semals were at the level of his shoulder, and when he had folded his handkerchief and his beret for a pad he slid the tub a half-length forward.

"Take care, Alain."

"Monsieur Alain, you are not going to carry that semal?"

"Alain, take care."

"He will drop it."

"It is too far."

"It is too heavy."

"He will rupture himself."

273

"Take care, Alain."

"Monsieur Alain, you are not going to carry that semal?"

"Alain, take care."

"He will rupture himself."

"Joan Antoni ruptured himself, falling with a semal."

"You are not used to it, Monsieur Alain: leave it to the men."

"Take care, Alain."

"Take care."

"He will burst."

Madeleine was taking crushed bunches out of the tub to ease the weight.

"I'll carry it with you," said Côme. "But there's no need. They will be coming up presently. What we ought to have is a mule: they have got a mule over there."

Alain worked the tub forward on to his left shoulder: it was an oval tub with two downward-sloping handles, six inches of branch that the cooper left on the staves. One was in front of him, the other behind: with his right hand crossed over his bowed head he gripped the forward handle, straightened and walked off.

He had done it before quite often when he was home from Paris or Montpellier: he knew how to do it. The tub was rightly balanced, leaning in against his head with its bottom edge cushioned by the folds of his beret: his right hand had hardly any work to do. Why had he remembered it as so big a load? And why did they make so much fuss?

There was a dead silence as he walked off, but as he reached the first downward turn one said, in a low voice, "He will drop it," and another, "He should have left it to the men." They said, "En Laurens and Pau are just sitting there."

"A whole semal. It will be wasted."

"He is not used to it."

"He will do himself an injury."

"He will burst."

The first piece had been easy. It was the flat, crossways traverse on the smooth, flattened earth leading to the first downward path. The weight was squarely above him, and it seemed as if he could carry it for half a mile. But now, here at the very turn, a long vine-shoot reached across his path: he put his right foot on it, but the vine grew on his left side, and his left foot caught in the arch of the doubly anchored branch. It broke, but not before he had staggered and nearly fallen. The jerk had canted the load forward on his shoulder, and though he hitched it back he could never get it rightly poised again.

On the downward path he knew why he

had remembered the carrying as a formidable task: he remembered, too, the strange pain of his blood-starved right arm, already drained of strength, though it had not been held up a full two minutes. How had he been able to forget it so completely? Now the recollection was so easy and complete; and he knew, too, that soon his breath would come short and the muscles of his thighs would tremble.

The slope changed everything with the balance: now the fact that he had as much as his own weight fixed higher than his shoulders — that he was utterly top-heavy — meant that every unevenness, every tilting slab of stone, could move the burden those few inches out of true balance that would start a big sway sideways or backward, a sway that he could never control once it has passed more than a hand's breadth either way.

Why had he ever thought that his handkerchief and beret would make a sufficient pad? Or had they slipped out altogether? There were seventy kilos pressing into the bony top of his shoulder, all the weight concentrated into the sharp rim of the semal. Pau and En Laurens had thick pads of sacking and a strap.

Lord, he said, what a stupid way of carrying grapes: one's body is at an absurd mechanical disadvantage. Sweat ran into his eyes, and while he was blinking them clear his foot went down into a hole. With both knees bent he took the jar, forced the weight back to the upright: but too far, he had wrenched it back too far, and now it was slowly swaying backward, bearing him backward on his heels. He gripped with his toes, quite silent in his mind, deaf, and oblivious to everything but the necessity of mastering the sway.

It was true again. He was standing square on both feet, the weight perpendicularly above him. But that short moment of intense struggle had meant a prodigious expenditure of strength, and when he began to move again it was with an uncertain, shambling pace.

So soon: his knees were trembling already and he had not reached the bottom of the first stone path. How had he ever thought the tub was light? Now an easy stretch; but still the balance was not right; he had never got the semal well placed again from that first stumble, and now his right hand, instead of resting easily against the handle, just to steady it, had to be gripping, forcing the weight inward; and it had no strength in it.

The end of the first path: now two steps

up to reach the second. The first step done: but at the second his knee would not straighten, could not raise the load. He paused a minute, breathing hard, bowed over the step, dripping sweat upon the stone: then, cautiously, he changed his feet: the other knee would do it, could just do it driven hard; and he was on the broader, smoother second path.

But the relief was too late: he had spent so much in getting there that it seemed as hard as the steep path down. How the world closed in: no sound, no sight, no sun: the whole world was made up of the load, the pain of his arm and his shoulder, and the three feet of path that lay under his eyes. Plod, plod, plod. He made fifty counted paces. He tried to hitch the semal to a better stance, but his hitch only jerked his breath out: the tub seemed rooted in his shoulder, would not shift.

On: on. His knees were bending now and he staggered on the path. He cast a haggard glance around for a wall against which he could rest the hateful tub. There was no wall. There was nothing in sight but green and the path: he was a long way from the casot; a terribly long way.

Another twenty. Could he manage another twenty?

They could see him now from the top: he appeared from that distance to be going quite well; his perpetual deviations from the straight line and his tiny shuffling paces could not be seen from there. His face could not be seen, either, deathly pale under the dust, fixed, eyes exorbitant, no conscious expression of any kind, a face of intense and beaten suffering.

"He has not dropped it yet."

"He will drop it soon."

"I wish he may not fall and do himself an injury."

"Joan Antoni fell and ruptured himself with a semal."

"If he falls he won't have to pay any doctor's bills, ha, ha," said Côme.

"Why don't you run down and help him?" said Madeleine, with uncommon anger in her voice. They looked curiously at her.

"Oh he's all right," said Côme.

Somehow he had come to the casot: he had not fallen yet, though his legs were ungovernably weak. He could see the casot coming and going through the blackness that swept to and fro — the flow of his blood was a torment of which he was dimly aware — but could he make ten paces more? And worse, the well-trodden, smooth, and beaten path narrowed when it reached the little house, dipped and curved in a sudden downward run as it went round to the loading place.

Now he was on the slope: the great oppression hurried his unwilling feet; now surely he was going. But the roaring in his ears was the voice of En Laurens on the one side and Pau on the other: they were lifting the semal off his shoulder. Oh the blessed, blessed relief: quite suddenly his humanity flooded back over him as he stood there trembling, shaking uncontrollably.

"You should not have done it," En Laurens was saying, in an excited voice.

"You should have left it to us," said Pau.

"You might have dropped it."

"You aren't used to it."

"You might have hurt yourself."

"It's all a question of habitude."

"Fortunately it was not a big semal."

He said, "Oh well, it's done," and sat down on an upturned tub. After a moment the worst had passed and he lit a cigarette. It would be ostentatious to talk casually now, he thought. But as casually as his shaking voice could speak he said, "The Carignan is almost finished now." And "Have you tried the degree yet? It should make a good fifteen."

He said that he could take up an empty

tub, but they cried out that they would do it. They explained why they had been kept: the headband of the harness they wore for carrying the semals upon their backs (the carrying on one shoulder being too heroic for the whole long day) had broken at the rivets. They would carry up the semals, they said, and they piled three into one and started up the hill. He plunged his head into the cistern, and then with some obstinacy he picked up an empty tub — though the smallest he could find — and followed after.

He could carry it now slung in front of him, and he could put it down whenever he chose. He often put it down. And on the way he found his beret: it had slipped out, then. It had gone at that first violent hitch.

Halfway up he sat down and rested: he felt as if he had just got up from four days' fever; the trembling went on and on. When he reached the top he was glad they were all working again, for he felt the need of silence: yet one thing he heard — it was Madeleine's lower neighbor muttering to her "He brought up another semal." That pleased him, but he did not look.

He set to mechanically, going along much bent: he could still feel that glorious relief from the weight: but Lord, it had drained him. Snip snip, the cutters all through the rows, and the voices ordinary now; but he still felt apart, and battered. He came to a vine already stripped, and then another: almost every other vine was done before him. Even so, he could only just keep up: they were working fast to finish the plot, and the voices were low and rarer now. Then he caught sight of Madeleine ahead of him, crossing into his row to clear him a vine. How kind; how very kind: and when she saw him looking she sent back such a pleasant, friendly smile.

The huge midday meal was over, had been over an hour and more, and now the languor of gorged bodies was passing. They were working a little faster again, high up on the side of the hill, so high that they could see the whole of the casot's roof and over it to the flat place where the cart came up to take the grapes away.

Dinner had been a repetition of breakfast, though on a larger scale with rabbit stewed in wine and an added dish of cakes. One of the little boys, overexcited with the pouring of the wine skin — that brilliant jet of wine that each in turn directed to his open mouth — lay dead asleep behind a bush, where they had left him, speechless, in the shade.

Alain had drunk his full two liters, strong

wine, their own, the very best, but he had not eaten much. It had made his head spin a little, but wine in the sun could never do him harm, and now he was feeling wonderfully refreshed.

As the torpor wore off hands that had been creeping began to fly again; the sound of the secateurs grew more continuous, and the slow hum of the voices rose to the higher screeching normal pitch. Xavier was expected in the afternoon, and the poorest cousin claimed to have seen him already, talking to the Gaudérichs in their vineyard a short way up the valley. Whether it was in expectation of his arrival or whether it was the stimulus of lunch digested, En Laurens and Pau went up and down the hill like men possessed of seven's strength: the whole year's wine was gathering, grape by grape, basket to semal, semal to the cart, and so down to the courtyard where they would tread it in the open troughs that night.

The end was in sight: there was a triangular piece cut by the path, then a rough square that ended at the edge of the shriveled maquis: when they reached the top of that it would be the end.

"There will be thirty-four semals this year," said Alain.

"There were thirty-six in nineteen

twenty-three," said the poorest cousin, who disliked him.

"He won't be here before the end," said Côme.

"Still, it is a wonderful year," said Alain.

"Lording it about . . . patronizing . . . ," said Côme in a low and discontented voice.

"Nineteen twenty-three was better."

They had reached the end of the row and they were spreading up the hill to start their backward sweep. Alain had to maneuver fast to stay next to Madeleine.

Now bend again and cut, cut, cut. A new back would be a fine day's purchase. But still the vendange was a wonderful break to the ancient world: the work was the same, so were the tools; the ground did not change, nor did the vines; so then the beliefs, the customs, and the frame of mind remained unaltered. Up here he could more than half believe that the ritual grape crushed on the last vine's foot assured the next year's harvest. Without any foolish mysticism of the blood he could feel a hundred peasant forebears on the loose and stony ground. That was not childishness, he thought. He straightened for a moment to ease his back and suddenly, because of the white sail on it, he saw the great sea that had been spread out before him, unseen, since the dawn. The sea and the vast sweep of coast, where the brown mountains round out in arms and promontories: there was Cap Creus; that was Spain. And the brilliant ship, that was the first of the Spanish schooners, up from the Balearics, shaping her straight path for Port-Vendres.

Bend again, with the sea shut out. These were new vines, with little on them. Maccabeu grapes.

"There he is," said the poorest cousin, pointing down the hill: but Alain did not attend, for he had seen before him in the next row to his a whole vine with every grape untouched. It was Madeleine who had done that. Setting his lips he whistled loud, the whistle that he had not made since he was nineteen. They stopped and stared; she stopped and turned. With a quick pace he was up to her. He knocked her to the ground. She fell on her knees, and crouching over her he gripped her hair and ears, pressed his teeth hard against her forehead, and in the surrounding cries and laughter he crowed three times, loud like a cock.

Chapter Nine

The feast of Saint-Féliu came always after the vendanges: it was not the feast of the saint, and indeed the saint himself had often attended it in his earlier, unhallowed days; it was older than the saint by far, and older than his religion. Yet there was an odd mixture of customs in it, some obviously of great antiquity and some that were apparently far more recent. For example, the inhabitants of Saint-Féliu wore masks, as though it were the Carnival, and the more cheerful souls would change their dress, disguise themselves as pigs, apes, and bears — most often bears.

"The masks are simply carried on from Mardi Gras," said Alain, "and that is a Christian festival, if ever there was one."

"You have an odd idea of Christianity," said Xavier.

They were sitting on the Place, at the green tables of the Café de Gênes, under the plane trees: the leaves were worn and faded now, yellowing leaves, and their edges were torn by the tramontane. Yet still the weather held: the perfect autumn days followed week after week, and although by now even the deepest of the cobbles in the streets were clean from the mauve stain of the washed-out vats and treading tubs, although the strong, heady smell of the new wine was gone and the very last vines were stripped naked, yet still the sun blazed down, day after day from an unclouded sky swept by the autumn tramontane. Even now, in the twilight of the day, the heat lingered, and Alain's pig-faced mask lay on the table in front of him while he mopped himself with his handkerchief: it was stuffy inside the mask. Xavier, indifferent to the heat, still had his on, a human visage, pink and white, with a simpering pair of scarlet, pursed-up lips. Through the holes his cold eyes looked strangely alive: he was watching the preparations for the dance.

He did not seem at all inclined to talk, but Alain was in a bubbling flow of spirits, a most unwonted merriment and restless energy, and he persisted in his speculation.

"One might say that it is fundamentally the Bacchanalia, don't you think? The Bacchanalia with a whole mass of incongruous accretions."

"One might, if one were brutally uninformed. Don't you know that the Bacchanalia were held at intervals of three full years? What do you think trieterica sacra means?" The utter stillness of his mask and the insipid painted smirk on it made the strongest contrast with the deliberate harshness of his words.

"I hate uninformed speculation," he added, after a pause.

Alain put on his mask again. "Well," he said in a conciliating tone, "I suppose one should leave these things to the anthropologists. But it is interesting, all the same . . . And the bears. There is the bear-dance at Amélie (it is Amélie, isn't it?) — most probably they are connected. I should very much like to see a bear. They say there are a few in Andorra still."

Xavier made no reply.

Alain continued, "But what I am most eager to see is this new accretion. When is it to begin?"

"The sardana, you mean? Soon."

"I wish you would describe the orchestra — there's Côme," he said, pointing suddenly with his pig's snout into the crowd before them. It was an outrageous travesty, if it was Côme: the figure was dressed as a woman, vast and flowing, as indecent as ingenuity could make it. It minced about, and from the roars of laughter that followed it it must have been uttering obscenity.

"Is it Côme?" asked Xavier.

"Yes, I think it is." Alain listened to the voice through the gusts of laughter, but the high thin squeaking, the traditional voice of the mask, was so well disguised that he could only tell that it was a man.

"Lewdness. Lewdness," said Xavier, in a low, angry voice.

"Oh, I don't know," said Alain, "I think it is rather funny."

The figure was approaching the tables, swerving erratically. It pounced on the waiter and squeaked, "Will you make me a little baby, Pierre? Just a little one, like Louise's?"

"Ha ha ha," went the crowd.

"Don't be shy, Pierrot: you weren't shy with Mme. Bompas when her husband was away, you know."

"Ha ha ha."

"Or is it that he has a cold? Don't say that the chicken from Paris has given you a cold, Pierre?"

The young man ran away from them, scarlet, back into the café, holding up his tray to give himself a countenance.

"It's not Côme," said Alain, delighted.

"It is not funny, either. But it was probably too witty for Côme: Côme's highest idea of wit is a chamber-pot. If you must have some kind of a classical parallel, why not pick on the Saturnalia? There was the same gross liberty of speech, I believe."

"You do not seem to be enjoying yourself much, Xavier."

"Are you enjoying yourself?" The voice behind the fixed simper was unusually bitter.

"Yes," said Alain, nodding his grave pig's face, "I am having a lovely time." When he had thought for a moment, staring into the crowd that filled the Place, he added, "When you know all the people, and when everybody is having a good time all round you, things do not have to be very witty to make you laugh. Who do you think that bear is?"

It was a fine bear, made of sacking, stuffed with straw: round its middle it had a chain, which it clanked as it danced. But the bear was suffering cruelly from the heat, and when it reached the tables it called for a glass of lemonade.

"He will never get it down without taking his mask off," said Alain, watching it with intense interest. But the man's head did not reach the bear's head, and he drank through a hole in the bear's chest, deceiving one and all.

290

"I did not think he could do it," cried Alain. "It must have been a boy. Or do you think it was old Ramone?"

Xavier did not answer, and Alain, feeling a sudden spurt of anger, said "Oh don't be so superior, Xavier." But Xavier did not hear him: he was drumming angrily on the table with his fingers and watching the men who were arranging the lights over the balcony where the band was going to play. There were several men, a whole knot of them clustered round the trailing cables, and they were bawling instructions to one another, pulling in contrary directions, tripping in the fading light, arguing passionately with the bystanders and the people on the balcony.

"They will wreck the whole thing," said Xavier, springing up. He hurried into the middle of them and Alain could hear his hard voice raised over the general medley of sound, peremptory orders, a sharp and decisive putting-down. In two minutes the string of lights was up and the musicians' place was lit: But it was very noticeable that the festive temper in the Place had cooled, and where Xavier had been there was silence.

Now there was a fresh disturbance, a swirling of the crowd at the far end of the

Place, howling and laughter: the musicians' car from Perpignan was trying to get in, edging its way among the people, and three bears and an ape were rolling on the ground in front of it, leaping on to its bonnet, mopping and mowing under its very wheels. The ape, in a flying bound, had reached the wicker basket on the roof — the coffin that contained the double-bass — then Xavier was among them. The car's horn stopped, the excited voices died away, and the musicians went on to their appointed place: among the bobbing heads Alain could see Xavier pointing to his watch, tapping its dial, while the leader of the band made his excuses.

On the left there were screams of laughter: the delight was returning. A man with his clothes on backward and a mask fixed to the back of his head, but still more disguised in drink — drowned in wine — had done something so very funny that the man whom Alain asked could not reply coherently, choked and helpless with the laughter as he was. Alain stood up to see, but there was only the man being led away by his friends, the inane head wagging backward as he went.

In the moment of calm that followed, a thin man, covered from head to foot in a black cagoule, stood in front of the Gaudérichs' table, to the right, a little way from Alain. He had chosen his time exactly, and the general attention was all upon him: and when he said to Gaudérich, pointing with his hand, "Is Naboth with you? Is Naboth enjoying the feast today?" everybody heard him, and it was clear from the hiss of indrawn breath that everyone had understood. Gaudérich himself turned livid: with a forced, uneasy smirk he darted his glance from side to side to see how many of his friends had heard.

It was Xavier's return that saved Gaudérich's rich and greasy face: he sat down beside Alain, and as he sat the first of the rockets soared up, to burst in an unearthly plume above the harbor.

The band was tuning: a row of oboes, long and straight, the double-bass behind, two trumpets and a bombardoon; and on the left, in front, a man with a tiny pipe and a tiny drum, the drum hung from the wrist of the hand that played the pipe while he beat it with the other: no strings, as strings; no strings at all.

The second rocket — whoosh and hoo-oo from a thousand upward-gazing faces. That one was red again. Now the third. Up up and hoo-oo-oo again, for this one was higher still: a split second's pause before the great blue star opened, burst, expanded, and the evening was begun.

Alain, excited, his perception heightened, concentrated, heard the distant tap, the rocket's fallen stick, and then the first shrill pipe screamed out. Quickly the people were clearing the space in front of the band: they were quieter now, and over the hum of voices the harsh shrilling of the little pipe pierced clear, unbroken, playing on four notes, a shrill, disturbing, warning scream.

"Is this it?" asked Alain, leaning eagerly forward.

"Is it what?"

"The sardana."

"Yes. Of course it is. What else should it be?"

The lights, all the lights in the Place went out: some fool had turned the switch, but the instant angry roar showed so clearly that the crowd hated him and his joke that the fool, having hesitated for a moment, turned it on again. But in the darkness one of the musicians had dropped his papers from the balcony, and while they were recovering nothing could go on.

". . . you forget that I have not seen it before," Alain was saying through the noise. And indeed it was his first sardana, for it had

294

not rooted itself in Saint-Féliu again the last time he was there. They had danced it still in Cerbère, but it was the Spanish Catalans who had brought it back to Saint-Féliu when they flocked over in their thousands at the end of the Civil War: and in his absence, the young people growing up with it, it had become as much a part of Saint-Féliu as the American vine on the hillsides.

There was quiet again: quietness and ex-
pectancy.
In the Place, naked lights hung in the trees
the leaves by them an unnatural brilliant
green.
Below, were lines of people, a square
people lining the Place.
The front row sits on the warm paving
stones — the warmth
rises in the evening and the stones are soft.
And there are benches. Behind, the others
stand;
some lean in doorways.
They are waiting the sardana.
Now the harsh tense vibrant screaming of
the single pipe before the music
and then the music. Loud discordancy
barbarous to an unaccustomed ear
unnatural intervals and time
a harsh high braying, crude, unripe.

No easy sweetness — here no dulcet
  chime
and thump, the nagging beat, irregular, un-
  meaning but not to them.
The first men stand out in the open
just stand there, quite indifferent. Some
  old, some young
and now three girls. Join hands, a ring
but hardly move.
And over them and through the trees the
  crying spate of sound.
An undetected change in rhythm and the
  dance begins.
Small life, dull shuffled paces and the faces
  grave
some faces grave, some talking, grinning
  — jokes
but soon are grave and priestlike — hieratic
  is the word — and firm.
The steps are forming now, the ring ex-
  pands
hands stretch out and others break the ring
break and join with hands, man woman
  man
are twenty paired — another ring down
  there behind.
Attentive heads, but what are they at-
  tending? Music? Are dance and music
  joined?
Or are these things on different planes?

The steps cut high, rope canvas shoes cut
   high
Eyes watching the opposing steps across
   the ring
Backs straight and high-held hands
the whole ring hangs downward from the
   hands
the puppet bodies hanging from the hands
and legs are hinged — the feet free from
   the bodies' weight play off the ground.
The ring is hanging from the pulsing hands.
Now down: the ring contracts
it is symbolical perhaps?
the catching, netting fish?
he does not care.
Then high again, and wheeling now
half this way then half that
moved by laws he does not understand —
   no difference to his ear
and high, the leaping clean-cut high and
   springing steps
unchecked by weight — a flying, levitation?
not ever seen by him before.
And heads flung high.
Of course the music and the dance are one
dull clod he was those minute-years ago
   (but richer now)
The rhythm stops
a brutal thump. No more.
The hands go downward, centripetal in

*a quick hard shake and now the pattern
    breaks
the fragments insignificant — a shopman or
    a sardine-factory hand
No longer priests.
The darkness and the shining trees are dif-
    ferent now
a flat awakening
How far you were removed
Up and high — pierced, saturated with the
    music, rapt.
Relaxed now
but still unsatisfied and hungry for the next
waiting for the single pipe again
Wait long and hard and here it is again
harsh shrill stab right to the middle ear
a jet of brittle sound and longed-for pain.*

After the second dance there was a long
pause and Alain began to collect his scattered impressions. He turned to Xavier,
saying "I think it is immensely . . ." But another man had joined them, and he and Xavier were talking in a low, animated tone,
their heads leaned close together.

"Immensely impressive," repeated Alain
to himself, and he took a pull at his drink,
but the ice had melted in the milky pastis
long ago and the drink was tepid. The violence that underlay the music, or rather that

ran through and through it, was not that Moorish? The deaf thumping of the little drum, that was, surely? He wished he had been to North Africa: there he might have found so many likenesses. But these easy voyages, one never took them. Even Cerbère, where this dance had persisted through the years of Catalan decay: he had never even been to Cerbère to see it, although that was in walking reach. Nor to Amélie to see the bears — or was that dance at Prades?

He looked out into the crowd: they were milling across the Place again, staring at the musicians, calling across to friends, horseplay, and little boys darting among the legs of the grown people.

"That is an almost pure Moorish face," he thought, looking at one man, yellow-faced, untanned in spite of the long summer in the boats; a dark earth-colored face, momentarily unmasked. "Of course, they were here for a very long time. When was it they were driven out? The Morisco villagers, I mean." He thought of the tall, thin Moorish towers in the land behind. "How vague one's knowledge is. How one forgets. But half the people here have Moorish blood: we have, perhaps. Xavier would make a Berber chief."

The band had drunk: they were passing down their glasses. They were arranging the next piece on their music-stands, changing their reeds, grunting into the bombardoon.

People were beginning to draw back to the edges, sitting down again, swearing that they could not see through those who were standing up. The music was going to start; but by now Alain was quite filled and saturated, and now, when the big rings formed, he could no longer watch and listen with that first absorbed intensity. But now he could see the little superficial things that he had missed before, the players and their motions, the fact that the dancers took off their masks (why? no answer came) and that even a plain girl looked beautiful if she had a well-shaped body, beautiful so long as she was in the ring, upright, held straight but supple in the dance. There were some who danced better than others; a young mason in brown trousers whose feet flew with such grace and true proportion that the music seemed to bear him up: it was he who was the leader of that ring; the inspiration ran from his hands round, and the girl next to him, who had danced indifferently the time before, was dancing now with all her soul, grave, concentrated, and anonymous — unconscious. Unconscious, that was it: once the dance was well begun all affectation went, no simpering, no coy restraint. Her hair was flying on her shoulders, and the ring went round.

If only Madeleine were there. Oh that would be a sight for God. He imagined her there, her hands held high, her back straight with incomparable grace. But did she dance the sardana? He did not know.

But of course she would not be there tonight, with the blundering wit of the town leveled at her: she would be at home, in that dismal house behind the angle of the wall. The Fajal men were there and women too: Pou-naou and Dominique he had already seen — just little dominoes, quite recognizable.

There was no room for all the dancers now: they were forming inner rings, concentric rings; and in the middle three alone: all dancing with abandoned gravity.

Xavier had gone. The little man who had been there talking with him was still there, and Alain recognized him as Lesueur, an employee of the police. He was not a man whom Alain liked, but he was a civil little man — a Frenchman — and he bowed to Alain, making some commonplace remark about the dance.

"Where is Maître Roig?" asked Alain when he had replied.

"You did not hear him?" said the man.

"No, not at all."

"I thought as much, though you nodded at the time. He has gone to the scene of the murder."

"I do not follow you."

"But surely . . . did you hear nothing of what he said, then?"

"No."

"I thought you were very calm. He told you the whole thing and said he would come back. So you heard nothing?"

"Nothing at all."

"Well, seeing that he told you there can be no harm in my repeating it. So you were not paying attention all the time." This seemed to fascinate Lesueur. He hitched his chair nearer, and leaning over the table he said, "He must have thought you were listening, of course. But all the time you were absent — distrait, as I might put it." He had a curious air, this little man in civilian clothes, unmasked and ordinary, yet as strange among all those fantastic garments as if he were the one sole man disguised. Leaning still farther over, so that his breath was in Alain's half-averted face, he shaded his mouth with his hand and said, "A fellow has stabbed his wife's lover."

"Am I wanted?" asked Alain, with his hands on the arms of his chair.

"Oh no," said Lesueur with a smile. "He made a thorough piece of work."

"Who?"

"Nadal, Etienne; rue de la Victoire. He was found by the husband, Batlle, Abdon, and killed in the very act."

"En Sin-bargonya in the carrer dels Mors," muttered Alain, translating rapidly: yes, he knew all about that. A sudden thought crossed his mind. "But he had lost his leg?"

"Yes," replied Lesueur, "the dead man had a wooden leg." With precise and disapproving solemnity he added, "That is what rendered the situation so indelicate."

The music swelled up, harsh and menacing: it was hard and bitter music and Alain felt the horrible inconsistency of the wretched wooden leg — the inconsistency was underlined. High tragedy, the furious boiling of emotion . . . but the wooden leg. Lesueur was saying "I believe we shall have to congratulate Monsieur le Maire very shortly now."

"You mean for his re-election?"

"No," said the little man, smirking archly,

303

"I mean the happy event: the young lady's case went through this morning — very quietly: no fuss or opposition. Five minutes. But he has told you, of course."

The refrain was beginning again and the rings spread out; this was the faster dancing, and the faces in the ring were shining under the naked lights.

Xavier had slipped back unseen into his place: he had been there for some time, for he had drunk his cognac and resumed his mask. Finding him there, Alain bent sideways across to say, "Can I be of any use?"

"No," said Xavier. "It is all in hand." He seemed happier now, well poised and confident; distinctly happier.

The refrain again, the last few bars repeated, then the end: the final thump; the hands went in, shook once, and then the rings were broken. Through the breaking rings, separating the last clasping hands, a figure came, a bear again, and lurching too; but this was the power of drink undoubtedly, for the lurching, staggering, swooping pace was not the formal lumbering of a feast-time bear. It had no train of friends behind it, no feigned keeper with a cardboard club; and it was clearly searching, for it scanned the tables and the walking crowd. It swerved and staggered, swooped and nearly fell: it ran in a wide arc on the empty Place and fetched up standing as it saw Alain and Xavier. It stood there swaying, and for a moment it fixed them with a heavy stare, trying to make certain that this was what it looked for.

"Good evening, gentlemen," it said — it spoke in French. "We all admire your masks. But Monsieur le Maire must have a higher one" — it belched — "to accommodate the horns, you know."

It nearly fell, and bellowed out, "You are a cuckold: don't you know? You are a cuckold, mayor, old lawyer Roig. And Alain's horned you every night these three weeks past . . . three weeks . . . past." The voice faltered; and in the complete silence of the Place they heard it whisper "Three weeks past" again, before the hubbub of artificial conversation drowned and pressed it down.

The bear went off, slowly and with more even steps, and the pig's face and thc painted simper, rigid, silent, facing square into the crowd, gave no outward sign but immobility.

Chapter Ten

As he hurried through the dark and narrow streets the music reached him in waves, swelling at the corners of the downhill alleys, dying as he passed them. It was the jiggety-jig of common dancing now: the sardana was over, and now the whole Place was a slow whirlpool of joined couples, shuffling round and round and round.

He had left the café after half an hour, a half-hour in which they both sat silent, motionless behind their impassive masks. He had said good night to Xavier, who had made no reply; and he had said good night as he passed the noisy table where his other cousins sat. At the corner of the little street that first led up the hill he had stopped a lurking boy, young Joan Escampeyrou, and whipping off the boy's stockinet bag he had clapped on his own pig-mask in its place. So now he had a plain black bag with eyeholes, covering his face entirely.

In the streets there was no light: here and there, far spaced, there was an arched bulb which made the darkness stronger, but in the streets no windows lit, no open doors, no golden chinks behind the shutters. As he passed through the arcades it was like a village that had died, for here the sound was quite shut out, and the soft padding of his espadrilles was clearly to be heard. Even the cats moved strangely, flitting like wild creatures across his path, coming from the darkest pools of shadow and vanishing into them again.

But here at the corner were two lovers clasped, motionless and silent, bolt upright. Before he could distinguish what they were his heart beat loud for a moment; then he smiled. I must take care of them on the wall, he said. But the wall was quite deserted.

It was warm up there: the setting sun had swallowed up the wind, and the night was as still as a pall. It had been cold in the tower, where the sun had not pierced for seven hundred years, and going up the winding stairs he had shivered with the chill of those centuries on his back. But on the ramparts the heat welled up: it came from all directions, and even through his shoes he felt the warmth.

He was leaning now on the inward side, making certain of his bearings: he knew the place and every inch of it, but he wanted to be certain twice. That flood of light was the Place, of course: it was a waltz they were playing now, tweedle-dee, tweedle-dee, tweedle um-tum-tum. How they would be spinning, down there beneath the trees. Would Xavier be dancing? Custom and civility demanded it.

Then that dim, half-seen light was the averted church-tower clock: yes, he had been exactly right, and twenty paces to the left along the wall would bring him to the angle.

There was no hint of light behind the shutters in any of the houses as he went cautiously along the wall. Once a dog barked, but not with any urgency: once a pair of cats rushed yowling in the dark street below: but there he was, and undisturbed, on the corner of the wall, a flat angle without a tower, leaning over, within a whisper's reach of her roof.

He stared through the darkness at the house, and an English verse ran through his head, an insistently recurring verse.

> He set her on a milk-white steed,
> And himself upon a gray:
> And he never turned his face again
> But he bore her quite away.

He had learned it from his grammar when he was learning English first; and at that time, the language being almost unknown to him, he had discovered a beauty and a poignance in it that perhaps an Englishman would never have detected. The beauty and the poignance were perhaps no integral part of the verse: perhaps they were the product of the mystery of the language and the unfamiliar rhythm. But still the verse lodged deep in his mind (he neither knew nor had looked for the beginning or the end) and still it haunted him; and now he repeated it again.

> He set her on a milk-white steed,
> And himself upon a gray:
> And he never turned his face again
> But he bore her quite away.

"It certainly borders upon the ridiculous, however," he added, after a pause.

But there was no light in the house: it was dark, closed-in, and shuttered; and it had a repellent air of complete withdrawal. He could not see a shutter, no target for the little stones he carried in his hand. And until he remembered that this was the blind side of the house he stood and wondered, revolving schemes of leaping to the roof — too far, uncertain, no retreat. But farther round the angle, at the beginning of the straight again, he would have a sideways view of the house's other face: and now his eyes, wide open like a night bird's, could see the tracing of a shutter lit.

He threw a stone: but he might have thrown it into a well of darkness. He never heard it land. It was his aim that was at fault, no doubt, for it was a difficult throw, oblique and in the night. As well as that his heart was beating high, and as he leaned on the parapet he felt his arm trembling, although it was not cold. More carefully he threw a handful all together: this time they rattled on the wood. They rattled on the shutter, but that was all; no motion in the house, and behind the window no movement of the light.

Well: he should have known that. So many, many times she must have heard the pebbles in the night: she would not open for an unknown fling of gravel. Yet still he tried again: with no result. Was she asleep? For a long time he waited. There was one untiring cricket in a crevice in the wall, and far away behind an owl was hunting through the olive trees and vines.

No, she was not asleep. She was singing very softly, and there was a creaking on the stairs. The song was a little louder: she had certainly come up the stairs. He strained, but he could not catch the words. A flamenco song, profound and sad, with those long falling half-tone quavers. She had come much nearer to the window now.

> "A la mar fui por naranjas,
> Cosa que la mar no tiene . . ."

He threw another stone, and the singing stopped, cut off. Far from the Place came the sound of laughter. Another stone, a handful more: but the shutters still were closed.

"The roof is the only thing," he said, and he measured the distance down. A shocking drop, as far as he could judge. He lit a match, which made a round of light and showed the velvet outer darkness pressing in. He should have brought a torch, he said, as he swung himself up to the parapet.

He sat with his feet dangling over the emptiness a moment, and then considered all the plan again. "Why, you fool," he said, "why not go and tap at the door like any Christian?"

Down the dark tower and the steps: how still it was. Here was the door. He rapped.

"Who is it?" she asked, above.

"Alain," he whispered. He whispered it, ludicrously, through the letterbox. Pyramus with a ferro-concrete wall.

"Who?"

"Alain Roig."

Steps on the stairs: the door went just ajar, most cautiously. "Who?" she said again.

"Alain."

"Oh," she said — a doubtful Oh. But she appeared there in the wider gap. With an automatic gesture Alain raised his hand; but finding neither hat nor cap but bag it faltered, at a loss.

"Alain?" she said again.

"Yes." He had the bag off now. "I beg your pardon for coming at this time, but . . . Please may I come in?"

They were talking in whispers; and in the distance the music came booming through the darkness.

"Have you just come from the feast?" she asked, still not retreating from the door.

"Oh, I am not drunk or fooling, I assure you, Madeleine," he said, with a sober vehemence that carried force.

"No. No, I did not think for a moment that you were," she said with a nervous laugh. "But you see, it is so awkward, with this divorce and . . . You will excuse me, won't you please? We will meet tomorrow."

"The divorce is through."

"Oh my God," she said.

Then after some time she said in a low voice, "I am so sorry I cannot ask you in just now."

"Then please come out with me. It is so important. I must talk to you, Madeleine." He felt the sudden grip of despair as she hesitated still.

"Is it really so important? Would it not do tomorrow? The morning is so nearly here."

"No. Please, *please,* Madeleine. I have to talk to you now." Was it all going to fall to pieces?

She reached back and blew out the lamp. "Where shall we go?" she said. He was irradiated with instant happiness, and he said "Thank you. Oh thank you very much."

He took her arm and they went slowly, feeling their way through the dark. Out of nothing she said, "This evening someone was throwing stones against my window. You expect it on a night like this."

Alain said, "I threw the stones. I have been up there on the wall for a long time, wondering how to reach you."

They went a few more steps in silence, and Alain said, "Let us go up on to the wall. We cannot wander among all the people in the town."

Up the pitch-black steps he led her by the hand, and they were on the rampart, leaning side by side against the inner wall.

For some time they were silent. Alain had not thought he could be so moved: he tried hard to control his throat, but when he spoke his voice was trembling. He said "I wanted you to marry me, you see . . ."

He felt a moment of the most acute embarrassment, and then he said, almost angrily, "I am not playing with emotion, on my word. I love you, I love you, Madeleine. I cannot find the words. But marry me: please marry me." The tumult of his spirits rose, almost to choke him.

". . . walk along the wall," she was saying.

In the darkness, as they paced slowly from the tower, arm linked in arm, his voice came, surprisingly close to her ear, "It would be such a kindness, don't you see? I do admire you so."

Silence. Then desperately, "I know you can hardly feel any strong romantic emotion about a man like me. But I would make no demands."

She pressed his arm: but she said nothing, and when they had walked a long way he said, almost conversationally now, "In Prabang there is the forest — trees of crimson flowers. And the people wear blue cotton and huge mushroom hats: they are the kindest people in the world. In the garden of the bungalow there are mango trees and durriens. And orchids. Prithiane is not far away, and there are all kinds of shops. My colleagues are all charming men, and some of them have wives. There is Tianou for holidays and the bad weather — that is very much more Chinese: you can get jade and silk in the Chinese shops, and there is the Malay bazaar, where the Arabs come. Lacquer. In the harbor there are junks and sampans: you can take a boat to Bali or Singapore. The old men and little boys fly kites."

They turned, by one consent, and went slowly toward the corner tower. He went on desultorily, describing the fantastic jungle birds and flowers, covering the unbearable suspense. Once she asked him what a lichee was. Suddenly he felt he could not evade it any more. "Still, that is not it," he said. "In this I cannot be giving: it is you that must do that, and I beg and pray that you will. I am so lonely there: and now I love you. I think it would break my heart to go back, living there alone." He had been impelled to this: it was the decisive step, and now he wished it all unsaid. The cruel beat of time stretched out and out.

"And Xavier?" she said.

"No promise made to him?"

"No. No promise. But you know . . ."

"I know. Poor devil. But the thought of you and Xavier makes my very soul revolt. I am not betraying him, I promise you. I told him that it was wicked to try to force your mind. He knows exactly what I think."

"He has been very kind to me, very kind. But I am afraid of him. And I am so very sorry too . . . He watches me from up here sometimes. I have seen him in the moonlight on the wall." Her hand was beating on his sleeve in desperate agitation. "And there is your family. Madame Margot. I could not do it, Alain."

He leaned her against the wall: there were tears upon her cheek, and he felt the fragility of her shoulders in his arms.

"We can go to Marseilles and take the boat from there," he said. The ebullience in his chest was painful now, the happiness oppression almost more than he could bear.

"I was a half-dead man until this last month past," he said; and vividly he recalled the sweetness of her forehead in the vineyard on the hill.

Silently they stood there, pressed as if they could never move again. Descending, his mind ranged furiously over the immediate needs of the next few hours. "We must go tonight," he said, "and go while it is dark. You pack your things — pack just what you need and I will get a car. Côme's car, I think. At dawn we shall be beyond Narbonne. Oh Madeleine, thank God you came. I love you so."

"Dear kind Alain: I love you too."

Chapter Eleven

It was warm in the hotel: outside, the mistral was driving sparse flecks of rain and sleet horizontally over the glistening black roadway and the people on the pavements were bowed wretchedly against it. By the force of contrast their room seemed even more agreeable when they came in from shopping; but even if it had been a calm and sunny day the room would still have charmed them. It was in a good hotel — good in the sense that the bed was comfortable and the people kind. Alain had said in the morning how much difference it made if the girl who brought the coffee smiled and said good day: and although the coffee was indifferent, he said he was happier there than at the Crillon or the Ritz.

They had spent the morning buying things, tropical clothes and books for the voyage, and the crowds, the hurrying in the streets, and the sense of shared activity had done them good. It had dissipated the dumb awkwardness and embarrassment that had threatened to envelop them entirely when the door of their room first closed behind them; and their lunch had brought back their poise — had given them an ordinary and agreeable level to live upon for the time.

It is almost impossible to be really happy at a time of very strong emotion, but now they were beginning to succeed: their voices were natural again, and they laughed. By a tacit understanding neither had mentioned Xavier that day, and now how many hundred things were overlying that unspoken name, taking away from its immediacy. And now the feeling of reality was seeping in — the feeling that the situation was *real,* so real that it could be touched and quite believed. For Madeleine it was as if she had been assured in the night that the sun would light the world; it was as if she had believed it, but only with her mind, not with her heart; and as if she had now just seen the first rim of the sun upon the eastern sky.

They were packing, slowly and without method: their bags were agape upon the bed and on the floor. A hairbrush and a rolled-up pair of socks, destined to be left for ever, propped open the wardrobe door.

She suddenly pressed a folded waistcoat to her bosom and looked at Alain's back — a look of whole-hearted, concentrated love.

He was bent over an open suitcase, ramming down a pair of shoes. "In our garden," he said, "there are snails. Immense snails. They come out when it rains. I adore snails." He took the shoes out and looked absently at them. "But Tran-Lhoc will never cook them."

"I can make a cargoulade," she said, and Alain turned with a smile, an open smile and with so much pleasure in it at seeing her again after that moment of being turned away, that she felt her own smile spread in answer to it, and a wave of fondness pierced her heart.

The shining black and upright Renault had been standing a long time outside the hotel: soon the policeman would be coming back with his angry words and his parking regulations. Xavier leaned over the wheel to look up at the hotel again: an unpretentious little place, painted white and green. L'Hôtel de l'Extrême-Orient. Speak English. At least it did not look like a bawdyhouse.

How much longer would they be? They were only there for packing now, and there was not much time to spare.

The hotel porter looked at him again. He took three steps across the pavement toward the car. But again Xavier's gray and haggard face, set in dark and savage lines, unshaved, menacing, and extreme, his rich and sober clothes, the Légion d'Honneur in his buttonhole, made the porter hesitate, stand thoughtfully and turn: the face, especially.

There was no other entrance: no, they must come out this way. But was it worth it, all this waiting in the cold? He had seen them going in — had found them in the last two hours before the sailing of the boat. He had seen their faces, laughing as they turned the glass revolving doors; and what had been the effect? Nothing. Nothing of significance. Just the statement, There they are.

All the way along the coast — that furious, unrelenting drive — his feelings had been clear enough. Black hate and rage, unmixed and plain: but had it not been conventional black raging, abstract hatred? Now (and he had seen them now) what was the truth in his mind? Was it only tiredness, hunger, and the cold that made this apathy? Alain had taken Madeleine from him; and was indifference the only thing he felt?

There was wounded vanity; frustration too, and the habit of revenge: but fundamentally what did he feel? Indifference, was it indifference? Was this cold and deadened sentiment indifference? It was like the ashes with the fire gone out.

And if it was, and if it was indifference, just mere indifference, then this was the end. If *now* he felt a cold dislike for her and him, if he had not the strength of feeling to hate them now, then all that he had felt had been a fraud: as Alain had said, a self-deception and a fraud. If there was no bloody hatred now, there had been no love before.

"Am I to blame, my God? Am I to blame?" he asked, and the hotel porter looked at him again.

"If I feel nothing now . . ." He stared blankly through the glass. "If I regard her with indifference — no more than irritation, then it is the end. But what have I done? What have I done?"

If he was not responsible, where was the justice then? For if indifference was all his heart could feel, then he was dead. And if he had died, all feeling dead, and yet he had not killed himself, where was the crime? Whose responsibility? And if it was outside himself, what hope was there? He had loved with all his power: and where was that love now? A punishment without a crime: a final condemnation without foregoing wrong. He stared straight ahead, an appalled stare through the rain-flecked glass at nothing, then he covered his forehead with his hands.

But still the jet of fire might light again.

When he saw them face to face, then it might blaze again and prove that he was still alive. They must be coming, must be coming: the boat was almost due.

He started the engine, made it hum, and the glass doors turned. He slid in the gear; was ready now. Yes, there they were; they bowed against the mistral as they reached the street, arms clasped, a suitcase in Alain's other hand.

He would let them go a little way ahead, then quickly down to the quay before them: that was the best place, open and clear. The plan had charge: there was no reflection now.

"What is the matter, petit chou?" said Madeleine. It was almost the first endearment she had ventured, and the continuing rigidity of Alain's arm made her wish it then unsaid.

"Nothing . . . nothing," he said, with the lic apparent. "I was — I was wondering about my razor. But it is in the little bag. I remember now."

He had seen Xavier's car and Xavier's back down the side street on the right. A shop clock showed the time — no time to waste at all. No cabs. The street running to the quay was dead, stone dead and cold.

Three cabs passed suddenly, filled with

late and hurrying passengers. A glance —
haggard — showed that they were no use to
him.

Madeleine looked at his face. What had
she done? Was he regretting it? It was decisive now, the boat and then no turning back.
Was she pushing herself on him, being carried along on his pity? The doubt was like a
hammer in her face. For a moment she
thought she was going to faint: he was a
stranger, and she could not speak.

As they crossed on the cobbles he gripped
her arm, and she felt it go numb with pain,
but the racing words hardly faltered in her
head. Oh let it not be so, oh make it not be
so, dear Mary Mother of God, pray make it
not be so . . . The enormous roar of the siren
almost engulfed the prayer.

They were on the quay, and Alain was
hurrying her along, going brutally just in
front, holding her as she stumbled on her
unaccustomed high-heeled shoes.

"By God, we'll take it as it stands," said
Alain, half aloud. Words of no significance:
his mind meant he would smash all opposition down. How? Speed and thrust, the pro-
tection of the crowd; the power of will. No
crowd. Only impatient sailors at the gangway's foot. Sailors, and the figure that he
knew.

He had left his car along the quay: he had seen three taxis send five men aboard. Now he was by the canvas-covered gangway, the only one: the only place. He shook his head to the question of a sailor and stood there, straight and dark, with his right hand in the pocket of his overcoat.

Here they were coming, hurrying fast along the quay: a sailor called again, and the last siren, hoarse and appalling in its nearness, filled the sky. They were hurrying: he could not see her face. A hundred yards to go, and already the sailors were busy with the gangway's ropes, the bridge that joined the ship and shore. High up, on the top of the black cliff of the ship's side, a tiny officer was shouting orders to the men.

They were coming nearer, nearer, half running, clasped together. Near enough now. Now near enough: now nearer still.

He turned away, filled with an indescribable weariness of soul. There they were: he did not care. The gesture he had planned would have no validity. He felt no hatred for them, not any trace of love, inverted love or plain: not even that remnant of affection that he might have hoped to find: only this immeasurable weariness, and emptiness, and cold. All passion far, far away and dead.

But he did not care: he did not care: he could feel nothing very strongly any more.

The tall black cliff had moved: there was black water, a widening gulf of blackness, between the ship and quay. On the high deck there were white faces: and the bridge to the land, the gangplank, was rising, sliding itself into the side. The hole closed, and it was gone. There was no more bridge at all.

About the Author

Patrick O'Brian (B. 1914), whose works won the passionate admiration of millions of readers worldwide, died in January 2000. In addition to twenty volumes in the Aubrey/Maturin series, O'Brian's many novels include *Testimonies* and *The Golden Ocean*. O'Brian wrote biographies of Pablo Picasso and Sir Joseph Banks and translated many works from the French, among them the novels and memoirs of Simone de Beauvoir, the bestseller *Papillon*, and Jean Lacoutre's biography of Charles de Gaulle.